ICE
Copyright © 2016 Hilary Storm and Kathy Coopmans

Cover Models: Dylan Horsch and Tessi Conquest
Cover Photography: Furiousfotog
Paperback Cover: Designs by Dana
Editing: Julia Goda
Printed in the United States of America

ICE
By
Hilary Storm
&
Kathy Coopmans
PROLOGUE

Loyalty, Duty, Honor, Respect, Courage, and Integrity... Those are six of the seven cores embedded into a soldier's brain when you enlist in The United States Army.

I remember like it was yesterday, placing my hand on the bible, while holding my other hand high along with my head, turning my life over to protect my country. Only, it wasn't yesterday, it was eight long, tortuous, agonizing years ago.

My reasons for thinking agonizing have nothing to do with the Army. I live it. I breathe it. My life is consumed by it because it's all I've ever wanted.

It's agonizing because here I stand in complete darkness as one of the first women to graduate from The Army's Special Ranger's School. Agony may be a harsh word to use. However, no one was more relieved than I was when the law was lifted a few years ago and women were notoriously approved to serve our country in day-to-day ground combat roles. Our nation has come a long way in allowing equal rights to women. It's about fucking time.

For two months I trained, barely slept, and pushed my now well-defined body to the brink of exhaustion. My dream is now a reality and my right to be here is embedded into my soul.

My mental stability was pushed to the limits, physical strength tested to the point of pain so excruciating that I was ready to give up, surrender, and dare to show them weakness, but I never did. I would've died first.

With the help of a fellow Captain, I pushed harder, became stronger, and passed. Yet here I stand, ready and willing to throw my dream away, all for a simple quick fuck. It's the stupidest thing I've ever thought about doing in my life and god help me, I can't control it, nor do I want to.

I've been in the desert a little over a month now, lucky enough to have been given the same orders as that same fellow Captain who encouraged me all those months ago to press forward and prove to myself and everyone else that I could live my dream and become who I wanted to be.

Captain Beau Harris and I have been flirting, eye-fucking each other since we first re-connected in this shit-hole country. Both of us pissing the time away while we wait for our Commander to arrive so he can deal out our orders. I crave the day we get to go behind enemy lines and destroy a substantial military target. It's a mission that should have been started weeks ago. The higher ups have been tight-lipped and they've been pissing me the fuck off.

Hence, the reason I need sex. I'm not a slut; in fact, I'm far from it. But hell, after training and now waiting for someone who should've already been here, I'm sexually frustrated. My pussy needs attention. It needs to be pounded, fucked, and filled with a great cock before I lose my mind.

So that brings me to core number seven... Selfless Service. That's the one I've mastered. Everything I do is for my country or for my subordinates. I don't do anything for me, it's just not allowed. Well, tonight I'm feeling selfish.

I'm Captain Jade Elliott of The United States Army and I'm about to break every single one of the seven cores I pledged.

CHAPTER ONE
Jade

"Fuck. You smell good." Harris sneaks up behind me, places his hand on the small of my back as he pushes me inside my tent. I'm the only woman out here. The men all share a tent, while I choose to have my own. It may be small, but it's mine. At this very moment, I'm thankful I chose to sleep on my own. I'm selfish, always have been. My upbringing made me this way.

I'm an only daughter who rebelled against her parents. They wanted a girly girl, but instead they wound up with me. Don't get me wrong, I can be as girly as they come. I love the feel of silk across my soft skin, and the smell of lavender in my bath, or my nails and toes pampered.

However, when you grow up with four older brothers who played Army and you wanted someone to play with, then you played it too.

I could carry on for hours about how I became a soldier. There's no time for it now. Right now, my pussy is throbbing, the need to be touched by a man and not my fingers has me spinning around and cupping Harris's already hard cock.

"Don't fucking talk, and I swear if you tell anyone, I'll cut your dick off." He grabs my throat when I threaten his manhood. He knows I want this. I need this. Hell, it's to the point now that we're both distracted. I'm hoping this is like a bad itch that'll go away after we scratch it and oh fuck, do I ever plan to scratch it. He wants this as much as I do. I'm tired of playing games and hell, there isn't time for foreplay, I'm wet and ready.

"Don't give me orders." His grip on my neck releases when our lips connect. Our hands both clawing at clothing with desperation and urgency. God, I want his dick inside me more than I care to breathe right now. How did I turn into this desperate pile of disgrace? I'm like a crack whore waiting for her next hit. I just need this. Right. Fucking. Now.

"On your knees," he tries to order me to position.

"I'm not here to suck dick. I want the real deal."

"Oh. You're gonna get the real fucking deal. You should be worried about how you're gonna stay quiet when I pound that sweet pussy all night long."

"We don't have all night. I want you out of here before long."

"Look at you. Already trying to get rid of me. Don't you think you should wait until you've had a taste?" He bites my lip as he finishes talking. I watch him. The lights shining through the walls of the tent light us both up enough that I can see his perfect chest. I run my hands over his biceps and slowly down his arms. I've masturbated to the thoughts of this man many times. Having him in my hands is not a let-down by any means. He's perfect. Why does he have to look and feel so fucking perfect? I know him. The real him. He's a pain in my ass every fucking day. I could never do anything more than this right here with him.

We fight too much for that. He fights for leadership, while I fight for approval. I don't need approval from Harris, he's always treated me as his equal. There are some who don't seem to think a woman should be out here, dealing with day-to-day combat. Why I give a fuck, is beyond me.

He wraps his arms around me and fills his hands with my ass, lifting me until my legs are wrapped around his waist.

"Don't even think about sticking that in me without a condom."

"You're really sexy when you talk dirty." He's such a smartass. Why am I doing this again? Because I need dick in my life, that's why. I have built up aggression that I need to work out and he's the perfect candidate for me to take it out on. He won't expect more than this right here.

I slide down his body while he rolls the condom into place, practically salivating at the sight of him. Damn it. All those months of him bragging, and he wasn't really exaggerating. I guess I should be thankful.

"Get back up here. It's hammer time, Sweetheart."

"You really should stop talking." I don't even care that he's annoying me. I wrap my arms around his neck and my legs around his waist and let him begin to slide me onto him.

"Oh shitttttt." He feels so good. In fact, he's the type I'll have to adjust for. He's gripping my hips and barely sliding the tip of him into me, just as I hear footsteps outside the tent.

"Captain Elliott. Report for duty." Who the hell is that? Who wants to die? Harris stills. His eyes widen.

"Who the hell is that?" he whispers.

"I'm busy right now." My words are a mumble as I pull my hips away from his and roll them forward, trying to get him inside of me. This is pathetic. Damn it.

The sound of the canvas opening shocks me. My heart practically shatters when a bearded man enters. His eyes widen slightly and I swear I see him smirk.

"I can see that, but you *will* report for duty immediately." His glare is snarky and he's demanding and arrogant as hell.

Without moving, I close my eyes and curse this man. Curse myself for falling victim to the weak bitch syndrome. I haven't worked my ass off for eight years to be taken down by two dicks in one night.

"I'll be right there." My eyes never leaving his face.

"Captain." He nods at Harris. "I'll see you in the morning." I watch the bearded man, who I can only assume is my new Commander, step outside the tent. I don't hear the sound of footsteps of him leaving, so I'm sure he's standing there making sure I don't take too long. *Shit.*

I slide down Harris with a new urgency. My pussy is begging to stay and finish what we started, but my heart and mind can't. I may have just fucked up everything I've worked so hard to do.

My clothes are wrinkled at our feet, so I rush for tomorrow's set, discarding my old ones as I move. Putting everything in place in record time, including my hair, I look at Harris one last time before I exit. My gut tingles thinking of the possibilities of how good he would've been.

He pulls my arm, drawing me close when I try to pass him. "Let me know what happens." His words are a whisper in my ear as he holds me close. Nodding, I leave him standing there half-dressed while I go meet my fate.

I step out into the warm night air to find him facing me. His glare causes instant guilt, and I know I'm in deep shit. I stand at attention and wait for him. Everything I've worked my entire life for is going to disappear. And for what? Absolutely nothing.

"Captain Elliott. Follow me." He turns abruptly and walks fast toward the only solid structure in sight. I follow him with a quick step until he closes the door to a back room in the headquarters building.

I stand in position, waiting for my verbal lashing, while he moves around the small room. His makeshift desk is scattered with papers and files like he's been studying for hours. I focus on my posture and try to keep the fear from showing on my face. My career is completely fucked, and I didn't even get to enjoy it as it went up in flames.

"On your fucking knees." His order surprises me. I've been disrespected as a woman many times along the way, but never like this, and especially not by a superior. I've always managed to prove myself to my unit, and the guys usually had my back in any situation that came up, even the ones who I know don't want me here.

"Excuse me, Sir." I'm desperately trying to shelter the rage boiling inside of me with my tone.

"I said. Get. On. Your. Fucking. Knees." My eyes meet his as I struggle with his command. Deep, dark blue, penetrating eyes dominantly sever into mine. What in the fuck?

"If you want to keep your position on this mission, you'll make me forget what I just saw you doing. There's really only one way I can think that you can do that." I'll never drop to my knees for this man. He can die trying to make me.

He's watching me as I process his words. That fucking smirk on his face makes an appearance again, and my hatred begins to grow.

"In fact, if you're good enough, I'll even let you pay the debt for your little fuck buddy, Captain Harris." Shit. I stand there with what I hope appears to be confidence, when in all reality, I'm dying inside. I can't degrade myself enough to beg on my knees for my position. I'm better than that. I know I'm done forever, but to defy Harris by not giving him the loyalty I know one hundred percent he'd have for me, isn't an option.

There's a very large grey area when it comes to sexual relations while on active duty. First, I could argue that we're truly not active at the moment. It's definitely something that's frowned upon with Officers; we set the mood for the entire squad, and the last thing we all want is everyone trying to fuck everyone else. Harris and I are both Captains, so it's not completely against the rules, but it's reason for reprimand, that's for certain.

"Unless you'd rather I report what's still going through my head. I mean, the images are burnt into my brain while I try to decide how to handle this raging hard-on you've caused." I don't move. I'm frozen in the position I've stood so many times, listening to the words that will change my life forever. I know this. I can feel that much.

He has a hard-on? For me? Jesus. What the hell is going down here?

He stops directly in front of me, his shirt bulging from the obvious muscles that are hidden beneath the fabric. That beard catches my attention again. It's one of the longest ones I've seen allowed in the Army, but then again, Special Forces has its own set of rules. He's older than I am, I'd guess by at least five years, maybe six. His eyes are demanding. I still can't look into them. It's as if he's trying to degrade me. This man is pissing me off.

"Captain. Don't leave me waiting." He stands proud as his eyes trace my body. This uniform isn't flattering in my opinion, but he obviously thinks otherwise. His stare has me aching all over again. My body betraying me in ways I can't express or begin to understand. Fuck, I'm confused all to hell.

I start to rationalize my options. I'm really not left with many. I can suck off my Commander and hope he holds his end of the bargain, or I can walk out of here, knowing my fate.

"CAPTAIN. ADDRESS ME WHEN I SPEAK TO YOU." The loudness of his voice startles me into a tighter stance.

"Sir, yes sir." He moves closer, inspecting me closely as he does. He walks all the way around me, close enough to inhale my scent if he wants to. Feeling him brushing my ass with his hand, I flinch and feel a burn from his simple touch.

"That's better." The breath from his deep voice hits my ear as he passes. He moves in close to my face when he finishes circling me. His inspection of my body is obviously over. I find myself cringing with the way I feel right now. My new Commander is a prick, and this is not exactly the best first impression for either of us.

"What's your decision, Captain?" His deep grumble is more than a whisper, but not easily heard.

"I haven't done anything wrong, Sir." The intensity in his face increases. He's pissed off, and I don't really know how to cool down this situation with words. I'm left with defending my actions and hoping for the best.

"That's subjective." I continue to stand with what little pride I have left flowing through my body, working hard to send the perception that I have more than is really there. "I can't have my soldiers constantly trying to get their dicks wet, or in this case, their pussy." That last word comes out in a deeper voice than the rest of them. *Why is that on the verge of sexy?*

"I assure you, I'm completely professional and you'll have no issues regarding me or Captain Harris." I mean every word I say. Truthfully.

"Ah.... Yes. I can trust that. Your legs wrapped around his waist and his dick shoved deep inside you. That's very professional. We could probably solve the nation's problems if we approached them with that mindset." He starts pacing in front of me, only taking three steps each way before he rotates to walk the other way.

I hate that I can't even argue with him. I hate that in the few minutes I've had with him, I've hated him and found him sexy as fuck at the same time. His demeanor demands respect, and it's obvious he feels I've disrespected him and will have hell to pay for my actions.

"Sir, we were in our own private quarters. The others aren't aware of our actions." He stops in front of me once again, his eyes flaring with anger.

"I could hear you. I heard him demand you on your knees. I heard the desperation in your voice before I ever saw it on your face." He moves in close once again. Why does this not get any easier? It's an intimidation move, I know this. I've been dealing with it for years; that's why it shouldn't bother me, but with him it does.

He lowers his head, letting his eyes trace my face. It's causing me to hold back a breath I very desperately need to take. He's too close. He's in my space. Maybe it's my guilt and the fear of what the consequences will truly be that are hindering my ability to cope with his intensity.

"I'm having you both removed from the mission." He rotates on his heel and walks away. "You'll be discharged, and I'll make sure your superior is very aware of the way you handle yourself as a Captain." The air leaves my chest in one long exhale. Did he not hear me? We did nothing wrong.

There it is. My worst nightmare. The exact thing I knew was possibly on the line when I started thinking with my pussy instead of my mind and heart. I love what I do. I've dedicated my entire adult life to this. It's not a job to me, it's my life.

"Sir. Permission to discuss in detail. Please?" Ugh. I'm not into being nice right now. I should have just shut my mouth and dropped to my knees.

"There's nothing to discuss, Captain. I'm here to make sure this mission is carried out without a single chance of flaw. If I feel you're in a relationship that will hinder your ability to function in that manner, I must remove you from the mission."

"It's not like that, Sir. It was just a..." I pause. How do I tell him it would have been just a quick fuck? That I'm horny and I need sex? Once I get my fill, I'll be ready to go for a while. I mean shit, there's so much stress and testosterone around me at all times, sometimes I just need to take it out on someone, then I'm good. My fingers can only do so much, for god's sake.

"Finish your sentence, Captain."

I swallow. Here goes everything.

"It would have just been a quick fuck, Sir. We won't let it interfere with the mission." His eyes narrow as he leans against the wall, like he's taking it all in. He takes his time thinking. I watch the smug look on his face while he processes the situation. He has me and he knows it.

I try my hardest not to look at the size of his arms bulging underneath his long sleeves.

"I guess this takes us back to where we started." The look of confusion on my face causes him to continue. "On your knees, Captain."

"How's that going to make all of this acceptable?" I ask while he pushes off the wall, slowly stalking toward me with a hunger in his eyes that almost equals the anger I'm fighting inside.

"I'm willing to make an exception to the rule in this case." He stands proudly in front of me once again, his eyes piercing through my sensitive skin, chilling me to the bone.

"Who's to say you won't out me, Sir?" I'm not dropping until he answers me.

"You have my word. I mean, you are the best in the squad, on paper that is. I'll have to decide if that's true for myself." It won't take him long to see that. I am the best.

My mind shifts back to the matter at hand. Why am I even considering? He's hot as fuck, so it's not like this will be complete torture; in fact, he has me wet just thinking about him using all that intensity on me. I can only imagine how passionately he fucks. The curiosity has me moving toward him. Step by step I watch his face. His tongue traces his lower lip, slowly, tempting me even further.

"I can even promise your fuck buddy will not be punished for his actions in this."

I watch him as I contemplate my move. Is this a test to him? Is he testing my dedication to this team and my career? Is he really willing to let me do this?

I swallow my pride and begin to kneel before him. This won't be for me. This is for Harris. He takes a slight step back and unzips his fatigues. He pulls out his very large cock, and I close my eyes, open my mouth, and I take him in as far as I can. He allows me to take my time for a few seconds before he takes a hold of my head and fucks my mouth with multiple precise thrusts, hitting the back of my throat each time.

He pauses, lifting my chin so that our eyes meet.

"Why did you go to your knees? I had such faith in you. With that record of yours, I didn't peg you for a little whore."

With his cock still in my hands, I lean back, making sure he can see my mouth as the words leave it. "Don't forget who's in control right now." I squeeze his hard-on with both hands, because fuck if it doesn't take both to cover it. "Don't ever underestimate me, Commander. I'm not afraid to do the work to get through my mission." And right now my mission is to keep my ass out of trouble. "Don't for once think I'm doing this for you."

His grin is challenging. "Get up." He lifts me up, faster than I intended, and has me turned around with my back flat against his chest. His hands move over my clothes, teasing my breasts, pinching my nipples along the way.

"I'm not beneath fucking you to prove a point." His voice is even deeper now.

"I'm not either." I try to stand strong, attempting to hide the nerves twisting through my body. He grips my neck with one hand, squeezing a little tighter than I'm prepared for, and I hate my body for loving that.

He slides his fingers between the buttons of my shirt, letting them explore my sensitive nipples. They don't lie to him. Hell, they're practically begging for his touch.

"You'll have me thinking about these bare tits every time I see you. I'd advise you to be more prepared the next time I see you."

My body shifts with his statement. More prepared? How can anyone be prepared for something like this?

He pulls my face to the side and grumbles near my cheek. "Address me when I talk to you."

I force out a quiet "Sir, yes sir" before he releases the grip on my throat.

His hand slides down the front of my body and into my pants, slowly going straight for the part of my body that's still sensitive. I'm practically crawling out of my skin with all the desire flowing through me. I want to not crave his touch. I want to not anticipate the moment when he will actually touch me there.

He finally slides his fingers over my clit, putting the perfect pressure as he starts to unwind me, making me absolutely insane as I fight my orgasm. It's not like he's doing anything different than I can do to myself. His strong fingers have me moaning inside. However, it's in this moment that the anticipation is killing me. The waiting to see what he'll do has me at full attention with all of my senses on alert.

"Look how quickly the control changes." My skin chills with his words. The depth of his voice continues to surprise me in the otherwise silent room. He has me on the edge with his touch, and I feel my body shift even closer to him, begging for that fall.

"What would you do if I stopped?" I shake my head, hoping he doesn't punish me that way. The irony of me thinking he'd be harsh if he stopped when just a few minutes ago I felt the reprimand of forcing me to kneel to him was horrible, isn't lost on me.

"Please, Sir."

"Oh. Now you beg." He slips a finger inside me, pulling it out, and then sliding in two deep into my wet, hot core.

"Yes, Sir." My reply drifts off because he thrusts his fingers inside me, rolling his hand deep to reach my G-spot. He holds his hand tight against me while his fingers move deep inside. I feel him exploring me, and I begin to crave so much more from him.

"Pants off." I move fast at his command, fumbling, letting them fall to the ground at my feet. He pushes my back until I'm bent over the table, then moves my feet apart with a tap from one of his. I brace myself against the cold metal and files, my aching breasts sizzling when they meet the coolness of the desk. My body prepares for him, while the sound of the condom wrapper fills the room.

Nothing could've prepared me for him though. His size is unlike anything I've had before. His rhythm is serious and demanding, and I love every fucking second of it. His grip on my hips will for sure bruise me, but in this moment, I'm ok with any marks he wants to leave on my body.

He fucks me relentlessly. I orgasm twice before he grips my shoulders, pulling me even closer to him so he can pound into me hard enough to bring his own release.

Exhaustion spreads through me. I've waited for this feeling for what seems like forever, and it was so fucking worth the wait.

He slides out of me, steps back, and bends to pull up his pants. I edge my way off the surface of the desk and catch a glimpse of the tattoo on his leg. It's massive. He has me curious, but I don't dare ask.

He straightens his clothes before he moves for the door. "Don't let me catch you fucking anyone else. Report for duty in the morning." Closing the door, he walks right out of the room, leaving me naked and confused all to hell.

Chapter Two
Jade

Oh my god. What the hell have I done? I just fucked my Commander. My warped mind let him strip me bare then fuck me hard. "Jesus, Jade," I whisper, bending to snatch my t-shirt from the floor and quickly pulling it over my head. Doing the same with my fatigues and my boots, I scatter my eyes around the room, making sure I've left no signs of evidence behind whatsoever. I'm out the door mentally chastising myself all the way to my tent.

"What the fuck happened?" Harris stands outside the entrance with his arms folded firmly across his bulky chest. He looks pissed. *'Well, fuck you very much,'* I desperately want to say. I don't though; he has no idea what the hell I just did, and he never will if I can help it.

"You don't want to know." I pull open my tent, letting the flap fall. For once, I'm thankful for the darkness all around me. I respect Harris, I truly do, but if he saw the look of disgust and disgrace I'm sure is plastered all over my face, he would know I've committed the worst kind of sin, broken every core commandment I've pledged.

"Damn it, Jade. I do want to know. This isn't just your life that may be drying up like piss in this desert. It's mine too."

I spin, ready to take my anger out on him, opening and closing my mouth several times before deciding to lie.

"I told him he caught us right before we actually started to fuck." Which in reality he did. Therefore, not really a lie. Harris is silent for the longest time. I know his eyes are slicing into mine. His stare is hard. Disbelief swarms the confines of my tent like a vulture swirling, circling before it swoops down to attack its already dead prey.

"Bullshit." His voice is low, dark, and threatening. This fuels my anger even more. I've been threatened enough tonight. No more. Fucking men. Right here, in this moment, I would give anything to hate them; however, the way my pussy is still on fire, clenching, trembling, and thanking me for quenching her thirst, there is no way I could.

"Listen," I say tentatively. Not because I'm afraid of Harris. I want him out of here. I need to think. I need to try to catch and hold on to every thought I can. My Commander, whose name I don't even fucking know, has single-handedly reeled me into a scandal that could cost both of us our jobs, if not our lives. And the bad part is, I fucking loved it. I've never been fucked like that in my life, and I know I'll always want more of the kind of shit he just did to me. I've always wanted a man who's not afraid to fuck me. I mean, shit, I'm not a damn weak bitch who will break. I need fucked, leave the making love to the other bitches. I've never been in love with a man to know the damn difference anyway.

"He chewed my ass out, basically called me a whore, and told me I was in jeopardy of a reduction in ranking. He went easy on me, Harris. Why? I don't know. I'm sure as hell not going to question it, and speaking as your friend, I highly suggest you let it go." His hand lightly caresses my face. I lean into him. His hand is warm, rough, and calloused.

"I hope for both our sakes you're not lying to me, Elliott." A chill runs down my spine, despite the dry desert night heat, when Harris removes his hand, his silhouette disappearing out of sight.

"I'm lying, Harris, for both of our sakes."

I've been trained by the best to be a light sleeper, to always manage to be aware of what's happening around me. Sleep didn't come to me at all last night. Fatigue mixed with exhaustion, anger blending with anticipation all makes a mean cocktail amongst my weary brain when I make my way from my tent to the dump, a horrific stench of a wooden box where we dump our waste. I may spend every waking moment with these men, demand they treat me like I belong here, but there is no way in hell I will take a shit or piss in front of them.

I toss my bag onto the pile, hike my backpack onto my shoulders, turn, and face the desert sun. I close my eyes, letting the intensity of the giant sphere beat down showers of heat even this early in the morning. Thank you to the maker of sunglasses. Tipping my head back further, I soak the scorching temperature into my already bronzed skin.

"Ma'am," Army Specialist JJ McPherson acknowledges me when he approaches. I tilt my head upright to stare at the twenty-two-year-old young man who is smarter than anyone I have ever met. He's a true leader, a sharp shooter like myself, and has been nothing but kind to me since my arrival. He stands at least two inches shorter than my five-foot-seven-inch frame. The little man can shoot a bullet straight through someone's skull from a mile away, I swear to god. I have never seen a more perfect shot than his, not even mine. That in itself tells you how much respect I have for this man.

JJ and I are the two snipers recruited for this mission; we've trained every day since we've been here. We're experts and have the ability to train other members in our team. Our capabilities are endless when it comes to every weapon we use along with the weapons of our enemies.

"Specialist." I nod.

"Apparently, our new Commander arrived last night. Came in without anyone knowing." He speaks as if he's excited to meet the prick. I could vomit my granola bar I ate while cleaning up this morning. I know all too well how our Commander "came" last night without anyone else knowing. The irony of those words have me laughing for the first time in days.

"Captain," nodding in my direction, our Commander makes his presence known. With a small tilt of his head, he acknowledges Special McPherson in the same professional way he addressed me. I shiver as the deep thud of his hard voice reverberates throughout my body. Standing tall, dead center of the doorway leading into the unobstructed tent where we sit to eat, visit, and hang out, is none other than our new Commander and the man I thought about fucking all night.

"Sir." We both stand at attention. Assertive posture, chin up, chest out, shoulders back, and stomach in, not that I have one. Head and eyes are always to be locked in a forward position. Without a shadow of a doubt, this is the first time I would love to flip a superior officer off when I raise my fingers in salute. Fuck me. And fuck him for making me feel this way.

"At ease," he commands. His demeanor gives nothing away to the fact we've most definitely met before. "May I have a word, Captain?" I shift to the at ease position and nod gratefully to Specialist McPherson, recognizing his dismissal.

"Follow me." He leads and I follow. My vision begins to explore his gorgeous form and Christ almighty, the wetness forming between my legs has nothing to do with how hot it is outside. It has everything to do with how hot this man actually is, and I've barely seen the front of him. I'm talking about his backside.

His shoulders are extremely wide, and I can see the definition in his back through the shirt he's wearing. Tattoos align the back of his arms, and I start to work hard at not staring at his ass while he's leading me. His t-shirt seems to be struggling to hold him in, and I can practically daydream an image of him ripping the material from his body in this scorching desert heat. Images of sweat dripping from toned muscle and who knows what else he's hiding under there have me preoccupied.

Quickly and without warning, he suddenly stops. My hands instinctively fly up, gripping his shoulders firmly. The ache between my legs increases, and I swear I'm at risk of my pussy exploding with the need for this man. It constricts, pulses to my very core. The heat radiating off him magnifies and sears into my hands.

God help me. I don't even know him, and here I stand with my hands wanting to dig into his muscular shoulders, slide them down the bulge of his back, and grip powerfully onto his tight ass.

Fucking hell. I've lost it. I need to be insanely medically discharged. It's not like me to want someone I don't even know. I sure as hell shouldn't crave him like I've never craved anything before. Then again, who could blame me after last night?

I step back. I need to clear my head. He can't know he has this kind of power over me. I will not yield. That's a mantra I've repeated many times over in my head. Never yielding to the enemy is engrained into our souls, practically tattooed on our brains. I need to treat him as my enemy. That's it, he's my personal enemy.

"Did you fuck him after I left you last night?" His voice is low. We're standing out in the open where people can see us. Is he fucking nuts?

"What the hell are you talking about? And shut your fucking mouth." He rotates on me. This man far exceeds the word handsome. He's beautiful. I've never seen anyone look as perfect as he does right now, all demanding and pissed off. I let his words sink in, and my insides shift immediately.

This is the last time he'll make me feel like a whore. I'm far from one, and I don't give two shits if he's my Commander, or not anymore. Not when it comes to this. He needs to shove those words straight up his ass.

Curiosity pulls its tight strings, rapidly firing away at my brain to find out this man's name too. My gaze lowers to his sand-colored t-shirt. There are no brightly-lit name plates displayed on our uniforms out here, ones that glisten off the reflection from the sun, making us an easy target for the enemy. Dog tags are tucked away under the confines of our shirts. No jewelry. We protect ourselves at any and all cost.

Therefore, names and ranks are engraved onto our shirts. We leave home to live in these foreign lands with very few personal items at all. Our entire life changes. When you cross a boarder into enemy territory, you live a new life. Some have new identities, while others lose their lives altogether.

CDR Kaleb Maverick. Interesting name. Mulling it over for a few short seconds, my head snaps back to the arrogant aroma radiating off of him.

His dark brown beard pulls my attention to his lips. I squeeze my legs together at the thought of what that would feel like between my thighs. He runs the tip of his tongue across his bottom lip as I'm staring. Fuck me.

"I asked you a question. Answer me." He smiles, those lips sending mixed signals. I wonder if he's ever been bitch-slapped. His arrogance speaks volumes. If he talks to women like this, I'm sure he's been slapped, but never by a bigger bitch than me. If we were anywhere but standing here in the middle of this unit, I would knock him clean on his sexy, tight ass.

"Fuck you," I snarl, my expression mirroring his. I smile. My attitude gives nothing away about the fact that I want to beat his fucking ass, except I want him to know one thing. The shit we did last night will never happen again. *Seriously?* My little inner devil voice screams at me. *One little—or should I say BIG—taste is all I get?"* I roll my eyes at her and him under my sunglasses.

"Look. I saw him standing outside your tent when I left you. If you didn't fuck him, then what the hell did he want?" He crosses his arms over his massive chest, those tattoos begging for me to lick them.

"He wanted to know what happened between us." My power of speech stays just that, powerful and to the point.

"And did you tell him?" His voice grows quiet.

"God, no. I lied." His brows rise, challenging me to continue.

"That basically if you ever caught me doing it again, you would make sure I lost my rank." I shrug. He begins to chuckle.

"Don't fuck with me, Captain. Trust me, the consequences will be much more detrimental to your health than being out here in the middle of bum-fuck-no-where-land. And don't ever let me catch that bastard sniffing around your sweet pussy again." With those nice parting words, he leaves me standing in the dust for a second time.

"Commander," I say before he gets too far away. He doesn't turn around, just stops.

"If you ever talk to me or treat me like a whore again, I will spit out every goddamn word you've threatened me with out here. I'll give it all up. Don't do it again, or I'll fucking ruin you." And with that, I storm past him. I hope the damn desert dust is flying into his slacked jaw. Fucker.

There are ten of us standing at attention in the blazing hot sun. Sweat dripping, bodies stiff, all of us waiting impatiently to hear details of our mission.

You can feel the rush and the overpowering smell of the desire to destroy and to make this mission our own personal bitch lying stagnant in the stifling air.

Like the rest of my team, I'm standing here listening to our Commander tell us how our unit has been handpicked, selected solely by him and the higher up chain of command for this special operations unit; how each and every one of us have excelled to be one of the best in our specialty we've all worked our asses off for, how we have bled, breathed, and even slept to become the best we could be.

I remain focused, eyes planted firmly ahead, toes pointed forward, until Kaleb stands directly in front of the small space between me and Captain Harris. It may be my own imagination, but something tells me these two had their talk and punishment has already been given to my dear friend. If I find out that is the case, I'll have to have words with my sweet Commander again.

"Captain Harris. Both you and Captain Elliott will report to my office no later than five minutes after dinner chow this evening. Do I make myself clear?" My peripheral vision watches as he turns his neck, waiting for both of us to answer.

"Yes, Sir." We both say in unison. I'd give anything to be able to approach this arrogant asshole with a few more adjectives addressed behind my appropriate answer.

"Now, for our mission. You're all well aware you've been brought here to complete one thing. Once we do, you'll return home to your families and loved ones. I really don't care who you have back home waiting for you. You all will return safe. I have no intentions of leaving any of you behind." He paces back and forth in front of us while he talks, his hands folded neatly together behind his back.

He turns, stops, and looks every single one of us individually in the eyes before continuing.

"You're the best of the best. I know this. I personally handpicked each and every one of you. I've done my research, and all of you came very highly recommended for this mission. I'm sure I don't need to remind you that this is confidential and this mission is of utmost importance. If I tell you to do something, there's a reason for it, so don't ask questions, do it."

His pacing reminds me of last night. Now, his black t-shirt is being worn tight around his bulging biceps, and my eyes are drawn again to the tattoos covering the rest of his arms down to just above his wrists.

He catches me watching and pauses directly in my view before he resumes his pacing in front of the team. He really intrigues me more than I'd like to admit. How am I truly going to be able to deal with a large mission if I'm constantly drooling over this man? Stay focused, Jade. Remember he's an asshole.

As he continues to talk, I get lost in him. I can't help it. His ass is so perfectly fit in those fatigues. I've always been a sucker for a man that's in extreme condition. His swagger is unusual for the Army. Normally, everyone is so straight-laced and perfect in their posture. He's more relaxed than I'm used to seeing.

"Follow me to my headquarters. I have a room set up where we'll be able to share the intel needed. At ease, soldiers."

I fall in behind the others and work to slow down my beating heart. We file into a small room with a few tables and the most modernized technology I've seen in a few months. Harris ends up right next to me, and we both watch the Commander, taking in every detail he provides.

He spends his time showing us profiles of the enemy, including any pictures available of their families. My heart aches at the thought of any of the women or children getting mixed up in all of this, but often these idiots throw them into our line of fire on their own. This is the way they were raised, trained to kill the enemy. It's drilled into their heads by the idiot cowards that lead this country. Some of these children are given no choice. You either become part of their military or you die. It's something I'll never get used to and thankfully being an American, I'll never have to face that in my own country.

"Name is Maverick. Before the day is over and this mission officially begins, you'll know everything you need to know about me." His eyes meet mine, and we both smile just slightly. Harris slides his foot over to mine and pushes on my boot until I turn to look at him. He wipes his mouth, mocking me, and it honestly irritates me. I whisper to him, "Shut the fuck up"... just before Maverick calls attention to me.

"Elliott. Did you have something to add to this briefing?"

"No, Sir." The 'Sir' comes out firm and loud. For some reason, I know I'm in big shit for that. I'm going to kick Harris' ass for getting me into this.

Maverick is silent as he stares in my direction. His eyes fall to my feet under the table where Harris' boot is next to mine before I can pull it away.

"Team dismissed for condition training. Everyone report back here at 1900 hours. Elliott, I need to see you in my office."

Shit.

Chapter Three
Jade

I step inside the small room again; this time, it's even darker than it was last night. He doesn't have the lantern lit and the sun will be setting soon.

There's sweat still dripping from my body from being in the sweltering temperature of the direct sun earlier, so I welcome the darkness.

"CLOSE THE DOOR!" The volume of his voice coming from behind me makes me jump. I didn't realize he was in the room already. Harris held me up after we were dismissed, and even though I was trying to beat him over here, it's apparent I failed. I follow his order before standing at attention while I wait for his direction.

He walks quickly toward me, looking angry with his mean glare and an obvious frown on his face. He stops directly in front of me. I mean, like one inch in front of my face. I'm not about to let him know that his scent drives me insane. There's no hint of cologne, no soap. Commander Maverick smells like all man. Pure fucking man. I stand solid, preparing myself for whatever he spews at me next.

"Do you fucking think this is a joke?" The snarl on his face is terrifying. I'm trained for shit like this, but damn it, why do I love having him this close to me? I'd give anything to be able to bite on his lower lip and dig my hands through his hair, but I won't. He has no idea what's running through my head. Like I said. I. Am. Trained. For. This.

"No, Sir."

"Then why are you teasing me?" What's he talking about?

"I'm not sure what you're referring to, Sir." It hits me then. Harris. Kaleb Maverick is fucking jealous.

He lowers his hand until he's touching me between my legs. All thoughts of his jealousy are traveling away with the dust. He drags his fingers across the front of my camos, stopping when he finds my clit, pinching, agonizingly and slowly before he begins to talk again. "This is mine." He removes his fingers, scaling them tortuously up my stomach, the other hand joining in, until both of his hands start to palm my breasts and flick both of my nipples into desperation before he breathes his next words against my neck. "These are mine."

He slides his right hand up my chest, allowing his fingers to circle around my neck. "This is mine." Then he tangles his other hand in my bun, yanking out the elastic that's holding it into place. His fingers pull harshly at the knots, sending slight pain into my scalp. He yanks my hair back, causing my eyes to meet his as he towers over me. "This is mine. I'm the only one who gets to feel your fucking hair as you slide it across my skin."

His touch isn't gentle. It's demanding, rough, and it has my skin on fire, burning and smoldering into an ache for more.

He flips me around to face away from him just before his hard body crashes into mine, causing us both to stumble forward until we're against the wall. The cool planes of the wall do nothing to cool the flaming desire I have.

I turn my face so that it's my cheek against the concrete. My nipples slide against my shirt with each deep breath I take. His hand glides down my body again until he's filled his palm with my ass. "This will be mine soon. I can fucking promise you that." His hard cock grinding into the crevice of my ass leaves my mind fraying like a nylon rope, my pussy pulsing, and images I've never even thought of before scattering across my fog-induced brain.

He's consumed me. I came in here with the plan to never let him touch me again, and in literally ten seconds, he has me begging inside. I want him to devour me, and I want to fucking devour him.

Our deep, desperate breaths match up as he moves his face next to mine. He pulls my lips toward his and turns me around to face him just before our lips have the chance to touch. He takes a step back.

I plaster my back against the wall, palms at my sides, and welcome the scrape across my skin as I move. Right now, I'm thankful for this wall. I'm not really sure if I would be standing without it. Oh, I'm shaking alright, quivering even. I feel my knees knocking, my heart is pounding and skipping around in my chest.

He's watching me; I can feel his eyes move over my body, while I can't seem to move mine from watching his chest sink with each exhale. Fuck me, he's just as affected as I am. He's driving me crazy inside as I lose the battle of standing strong against his advances. I know how good he feels, and my body won't allow me to even consider denying myself the pleasure he can bring.

"Take off your shirt." I move with confidence at his demand. "Bra too." I expose myself bare to him. His penetrating gaze shifts from my face to my neck, then locks onto my heaving chest. My nipples seem to beg for his command as they harden to an excruciating need of pain. I wait for him to say something. Touch something. Fucking do some...thing. Any damn thing.

I begin to fight myself internally, the need to be touched or touch myself driving me out of my ever-loving mind. I refrain from taking the step to show him I'm weak at the moment. I'm stronger than this shit. I don't need a man. I don't fucking wait for a man. And I sure as fuck don't beg for a man.... that is until him, but he doesn't need to know that.

He steps toward me once again, grinding his cock into me, sliding me up the wall as he does. His beard is soft against my neck as he trails his tongue down toward my chest. My once heated skin chills everywhere with his touch.

"What is your pretty little head thinking? Are you craving this?" He rolls his hips forward, grinding his bulge against me, sending my eyes closed and a frantic internal plea for him to do it again. He does, and I run my fingers through his hair and moan against his ear when he reaches between us to tug at my belt.

My pants slide down, and I kick my boots off to free my legs entirely. If that doesn't answer his question, then I don't know what the hell will. He grabs his own belt, tugs it loose, and I watch his sturdy fingers make a hasty effort to lose his pants. Son of a bitch, not only do I have one hell of a Commander to look at, I've also been hit with a man who wants to fuck me again.

He steps back again to watch me. Standing here completely naked is new to me. I've never treated sex any differently than fulfilling a need, then moving on. His stare is intense, touching parts of me that have never been touched. Inside shit that I'm not sure I like being affected... and it's starting to make me nervous, which is a new emotion for me. I'm confident in every damn thing I do, so why is it so different with him? He's not any better than I am.

"Why are you watching me like that?" I ask angrily.

"Because I can."

"What if I don't like it?" I snap. Why is he taking so long to move to me? Has he changed his mind now that I'm ass naked in front of him?

"You'd better get used to it." He's so fucking self-assured, standing there in front of me, stroking his cock. With a cock like that, he's sure to be confident. I watch him as he continues to stroke it and can't help but look forward to feeling him fill me once again. I know it'll be raw, hard fucking with him, apparently just how I like it.

I grow impatient and decide to move forward on him. My hands grip his strong shoulders and he picks me up until my legs are wrapped around his waist. He steps forward until I'm against the wall again, then slides his bare cock inside me. I gasp from the sudden intrusion that stretches me wide, but I love how he makes me feel as he moves inside me.

I pull back once I realize what he's done. I do everything I can to try to stop him, but my strength up against his holds no power here at all. "Fuck. What are you doing?" I plead as I try to pull away from him with my back against the wall.

"I know you're clean. I know you can't get pregnant because you've had the shot, and I'll be damned if I fuck you with a condom ever again." He pulls back before thrusting into me harder than before, filling me instantly.

"Fuck. You feel so fucking good on my dick. Just like I knew you would." Oh my god. The urge to scream claws up my throat. His name is right there on the tip of my tongue, and I'm fighting like hell not to yell while he fills me completely.

He begins to fuck me fast and hard with one of his hands gripping my ass, the other pulling on my hair. My back scrapes against the rough wall with every thrust, but I don't dare stop him. The burn of the scratches increases my sensitivity to him, and I can't stop the screaming from my mouth when I start to orgasm.

He wraps his hand over my mouth, never once slowing down as he starts to fuck me even harder. I bite down on his palm and he groans, obviously loving my reaction.

"Oh yeahhhh. I can't wait to fuck you when I don't have to hide that gorgeous sound coming from your lips." His words are a growl while he pounds into me over and over. My second orgasm hits and again, I can't control it. Fuck. His cock hits me perfectly like this. It's like he's angled with the exact purpose to hit my G-spot. I feel my inner walls tightening and pulsing around his length as he continues to fuck me with purpose.

"Fuckkkkkkkk." I try to pull back from him because I know I'm about to lose it. I can't control this level of buildup and know shit is about to get crazy. He pulls me closer, never letting up. Fucking me intensely and vigorously, pounding relentlessly into me.

He throws his hand over my mouth once again. "Next time you're getting a ball gag." I dig my nails into his back, trying to hold it all in. Fuck, I've never been fucked like this. He knows how to do this, and I'm pretty sure he's just ruined me for life. I'll always compare sex to this feeling right fucking here.

He groans a few times just before I feel his warmth inside me. He soon finds his release and slowly stills himself. That's a first too. I've never dropped my guard enough to let a man pour himself inside me. It's a control thing, and it's obvious I've lost all fucking control.

He holds me while we both steady our breathing. Both exploring each other with our eyes as we do. I fucking hate and love what this man does to me. Damn him for having this much control.

He lets me down, sliding his black t-shirt over his head before he tosses it to me. "Here, use this to clean up. Even though I'd love for you to smell like me, sex is like a weapon out here. It's as deadly as the scent of a woman. And trust me, Jade, your scent alone can drive a man to his goddamn knees." I'm frozen in this spot. His words practically paralyze me, but the sight of his tattoos shocks me. He's very naked, yet covered in tattoos on his back, arms, and most of his chest. His legs have a few and frankly look out of place on his otherwise insanely inked canvas. His nipples are pierced and I want nothing more than to run my tongue over them.

"Holy shit. Your tattoos." I'm lost in them.

"Yeah. I have a few." When he starts to pull up his pants, I just want to stop him and inspect every single tattoo on his perfect body.

Words fail me as my eyes try to take in everything I'm seeing. This is an unheard-of amount of tattoos for the Army.

"I can't stop looking."

"You'll have to, Captain. We have shit to do. We'll be here for days if you try to see them all. And if you keep looking at me that way, my cock will be hard again in no time." Oh hell. I'm intrigued now. I need to at least ask about one of them.

"Ok. Let's start with one. Which one is your favorite?" I question with curiosity.

"My MOM tattoo. Hands down." Awe shit.... he loves his mom. Maybe he's not the hard-ass he wants people to think he is.

"That's awesome. I bet she's proud of you for that." He nods. He doesn't elaborate or give any further detail, while I continue to stare in disbelief and getting dressed at the same time. There's something to this guy. His beard is longer than usual... and those tattoos are everywhere. Yes. They would be covered in a uniform, but there's something else about him. I'm dying to find out who is behind the mask of Kaleb Maverick.

"Who are you really?" By the way he arches his brow and stiffens his spine, I would say this question surprises him.

"What do you mean by that, Captain?" His tone is challenging.

"You're bigger than all the guys here. You're tattooed almost completely, and that beard of yours shouldn't be allowed." He looks at me like he's trying to decide how to answer.

"I'm retired. They brought me back for this mission. I agreed on a few conditions." Really? I wonder to myself. If he's retired, then how old is he? My guess would be mid-thirties. I begin to have many questions rattling around in my head. I'm just not sure if I'm buying his answers or not. I could call bullshit on his ass any time, instead I bite my tongue. I'd love more than anything to dig deeper into this man and find out more about him. Why he is the way he is and why his answers to my questions are short and clipped.

I'll find a way on my own to discover everything there is to know about Commander Kaleb Maverick. After all, he seems to know everything about me, personal and professional. All's fair in love and war, as they say. Even though there isn't a damn bit of love in what we have going on here. It's fucking and war. Primal, damn good fucking and hopefully a perfectly completed mission instead of war.

"You must be a badass motherfucker." His laughter fills the room. It's nice to see that side of him, even if only for a second. I'm not about to get my hopes up though, not when it comes to this man. He may think he holds all the power here and has all the control over me. No, I do believe my Commander has another mission besides the one he claims to be here for, and something tells me it has everything to do with me.

I make good use of the ten minutes he gives me to finish cleaning myself up after he not so formally dismisses me. I decide to clean up better in my own tent before I go anywhere.

Wincing from the scrapes across my back the minute I yank my t-shirt over my head, I try not to show any signs of weakness. It's something I do, never show emotions, even when I'm alone. I've suffered too much pain in my life, and it has no place out here.

I don't have time to inspect them though. I need to get back to our team, to train in these exercises he's demanding us to do. I grab a clean t-shirt from the wooden crate I have them stacked on, and pull it over my head and through my arms while I walk to one of the care packages sent. I know I have a supply of unscented wipes. Like Kaleb said, sex out here could be smelled a mile away, especially out here where the only scent you get used to is the smell of sweat. The distinct aroma surrounds you out here in the sweltering sun. A freshly-fucked scent would sure the hell have the guys picking up on the shit I've been doing.

"Captain. Let's move it." Son of a bitch. The deep voice of my Commander outside my tent sends a shiver down my damn spine. I ignore him and the way my body wants to betray me once again just from the sound of his voice. Unzipping my pants, I clean myself up and discard the used wipes into my trash. I tuck my t-shirt into my fatigues, pull my hair back into a ponytail, and grab a hat before securing it on top of my head.

"Ready, Sir." I stand tall and eager to feel the burn of something other than the sexual exhaustion he causes. I fall in line next to him as we make our way to the team, catching up to two other members quickly.

The sky is nearly dark by the time we approach our team all gathered around in a circle, listening to the second in command. He's an elderly gentleman with manners and respect, unlike the man standing next to me, whose eyes I can feel on me when we come to a stop.

"I thought we were training, doing drills, Sir?" I ask while keeping my educated eyes ahead.

"This isn't basic training, Captain. Physical and strength training will be done on your time, if and when I decide to give you spare time." He pauses, his voice low. I hear the sexual innuendo in his words. To say I'm not pissed off would be nothing short of a lie. My muscles ache to feel the burn from working out, this time not in the way he's suggesting.

"Captain, they're discussing Operation Mission Liberty and we will be doing drills. Night vision, military assault drills. Now get your sexy ass over there with your team."

"Fuck off," I mutter loud enough for him to hear. I march forward silently and carefully, joining my team and attempting to shut down my raging anger at both myself and him. How am I in this position? I did this shit to myself. He knows better than to show any sign of our actions out here, and him making comments like he is will pull attention to us faster than anything.

I listen and try to calm myself for the next hour as Major Roberts delivers our mission, knowing my defiant words pissed Maverick off, but he needs to understand that I'm not putting up with his condescending shit. I'm a highly trained soldier and deserve to be treated like one.

The mission is simple. Just like we all assumed, we'll be going in with our specialized skills, highly trained schooling, and our ability to be the best in a raid to bring down a very important enemy leader.

"The research has been done. The facts are laid before us. Azham-Amir-TajUdin is indeed hiding out in or around the small village of Tashraq, Afghanistan. We will capture him. We will defend our country, and we will all leave here in one piece. Report back here at 2100 hours and be prepared to spend all night doing these drills." Both Commander Maverick and Major Roberts dismiss us for dinner chow. I turn to leave, not speaking a word to anyone. I know I should eat with my team and socialize, but I ignore Captain Harris as he calls my name to my retreating back. I follow the urge to confine myself to my tent and pay no attention to anyone until Harris and I have to report to the Commander's office for whatever the hell he has planned for us. I will not let Kaleb Maverick ruin this for me by screwing with my head and leaving me vulnerable to the enemy or putting any of my fellow teammates in jeopardy. Fuck this.

"Damn it, Jade, stop." I spin around, ready to lash out at Harris when I jerk my head back. The look in his eyes startles me. He looks troubled. In all the time I've known him, he's never looked at me this way. Not even the other night when we were caught. "What's wrong? Did I miss something?" I place my hand on his arm.

"No. But it's obvious I sure the hell did." He steps back out of my reach. Those troubled eyes turn serious as a damn heart attack.

"What the hell are you talking about?" My mind is boggled, and I'm sure my face shares the same sentiment. If he could see it in the dark, he would know.

"You have blood all over the back of your shirt. Did the Commander do something to you?" He sounds pissed.

"Good god, no. Why would you even think something like that?" I retract my gunned-up response out of the blue. "I tripped over a bunch of ammunition and landed flat on my back." Just like Harris, I've been trained to be able to stare anyone in the eye and lie. He studies me to the point of an analytical evaluation, but I give nothing away. "I'm not sure if I believe you or not, but for now I'll take your word. If I find out you're lying to me, Jade, Commander or not, I'll end him." Those are my friend's parting words. I stand there in the now black darkness, my feet unable to move and my body shaking. I've never let anyone control my mind or my body like this. What in the hell am I doing?

What's happening to you, Jade? the sweet part of my conscience asks.

My entire military career has lead me to this point, where the rush and the feel of the blood pumping feverishly throughout my veins has my adrenaline hastily soaring. This is the second time I've let my Commander fuck me literally senseless. It's time I put a damn stop to it or this mission will fail before it even begins.

CHAPTER FOUR
KALEB

I pretend to listen to my team talk about the mission, while I sit here eating and watch her talk to that motherfucker Harris. He wants her, but little does he know he'll never touch her again, not the way he wants to anyway.

The moment my buddy Pierce Davis requested to see me in his office at his USSOCOM, also known as The United States Special Operation Command, I knew he was calling in his mark for him saving my life ten years ago when we were in the middle of combat. It was during our second tour of the Iraqi war. Without hesitation, I accepted.

Not only did Pierce and I serve for years together, he's like a brother to me, along with Kase Flynn. While Pierce continued to serve our country, both Kase and I had enough after serving twelve years.

We now run a tight private military firm, which is contracted with the government. Pierce and Kase are the two I directly work with to lead our team through the missions. I'm still serving my country by training or guarding significant military personnel who may travel in or out of The United States. We get called on special dangerous missions, and this is no exception to that. It feeds my craving for living the life without all the fucking rules of being in the Army, and I fucking love every damn second of it.

I know this country as if it were my own. It's one of the reasons I was selected to get this team in and out of there as quickly as possible. I know the process, the drills, and still have the desire to fucking blow the enemy apart until there's nothing left of them but a pile of ashes. Yeah, I fucking know the routine and can't wait to feel the rush again.

Pierce and I spent hours, days even, going through files, searching for the perfect team. I thought I had them all, until I opened her file. The blonde with the most captivating eyes I have ever seen. I swear to Christ those eyes popped out of that file and bewitched my ass. I knew nothing about her but her name. For the first time since I've met my military brothers, I'm keeping something from them. They have no idea I have a woman on this team. And they definitely don't know I can't take my damn mind off of her.

Captain Jade Elizabeth Elliott. Fucking beautiful. I scoured every bit of information I could find on her to the point of being her stalker. I'll admit it. I'm drawn to her in a way I can't even comprehend to my own fucked-up mind. It's fate, or maybe destiny, fuck if I know. All I know is she has fascinated me from the moment I laid eyes on her.

At first it was her outer beauty, then it became her drive, her determination to be one of the first women to enter and graduate special ops training. Then it became her agility. Her voice when I heard her speak in the many videos I watched her in. I'm obsessed, not to the point of placing her in danger, but to the point of making her mine.

"I need to brief Captain Harris and Captain Elliott on a few things. See you all in a few hours." I grab my tray, dump the scraps into the garbage, and walk past her tent. I pause when I step in front of it for a brief second. I can smell her. She's addictive. I clench my hands into fists and plow forward to my office, where I kick a few boxes over. My frustration at my own actions deepens.

There's a knock on my door the minute I collapse into the chair behind my table.

"It's open." I don't even bother to look up and see who it is. I know it's the two of them here to work their punishment off. One I have no damn right to give either one of them after the shit I've done, but as the Commander of this unit, I have to. Both of them need to understand. Jade already does, or at least she fucking better. Harris on the other hand won't get it through his head if I don't lay down a few rules somehow.

I would love to shove Harris' head in the fucking sand and tell him to stay the hell away from her, that she will never be his because she's mine; or at least she will be when I'm finished. But I won't.

I have nothing but respect for Captain Harris when it comes down to his intelligence, his ability to endanger his life like the rest of us, to kill a man who has done nothing but bring heartache and destruction to our men and women of the armed forces. The man can speak the native tongue of this country just as well as he can speak English. His ability to interpret is imperative to accomplish what we came here for, but after this is over, I hope I never see the man again.

"Good evening, Sir." Harris speaks. It's then that I lift my head, clasp my fingers together under my chin, and zone in on the two of them. Neither one of them will look at me. They stand at attention. Oh, how I would love to see him sweat. I may be a heartless son of a bitch for doing this, but I need to make a goddamn point to both of them.

"Captain Harris. The next time you need to get your dick wet, may I suggest you spit on the fucker and yank his goddamn chain. Fuck your hand. Fuck a damn hole in the wall. I don't care what you fuck, but you will stay away from Captain Elliott. Do I make myself clear?" The power in my speech backs up every muscle in my body when I stand to face him. Eye to eye. Man to motherfucking man.

"Yes, Sir," he bellows out his answer with no hesitation at all. He may think he has me fooled, but he doesn't. The man may keep his pin dick in his pants for the rest of this mission, but I know good and well he's been secretly in love with her for a long time. I know everything about them all. I dismiss him with my eyes and move to the beautiful creature who has enthralled her very existence on both of the men standing in this room. The great thing about it is, she has no fucking clue what she does to us.

"Captain Elliott." Mother. Fuck. My resistance wavers all over the damn place, my insides twist, my cock twitches, and my mouth waters desperately to latch onto hers. She should not have this much fucking control over me.

"Sir." God. I'd give anything for her to look at me. She won't though. She'll see this through. She's more than confirmed her loyalty by letting me have her. I want her loyalty to be to me and not to this man standing next to her.

"Are your fingers broken?" I snap.

"No, Sir," she responds.

"Good. Then the next time you feel the need to satisfy yourself, I suggest you use them." How I would love to be able to say use them while I'm watching you, or take those delicate fingers of hers and wrap them around my cock and guide me into her sweet pussy. It pisses me the hell off that Harris is in here, making me strain against my fatigues. The minute they walk out the door, I'll be doing the same exact thing I just told him to do. This is how much she drives me crazy.

I need them out of here, so I dismiss them. Neither one says a word as to their punishment or lack thereof. "Mother. Fucker." Sliding my ass back into my chair, I refuse to stroke my cock, not when I know what it feels like to be inside of her. The next time I stroke it, she'll be watching.

For the next couple of hours, I beat myself up as I sit inside my makeshift office. I've failed miserably in my plan to seduce her and to let her know I'm not just after her for a quick fuck. I had plans. I had two missions to complete when I landed back in this desert, and I have messed up the one closest to my heart. The other one is a damn cake walk compared to her.

One was to complete the mission that The United States granted me to lead; the other was to get the woman. I will complete the first mission, I have no doubt about that, but damn it, if I haven't fucked up getting her.

I knew the minute I saw her jump on Harris in her tent that I was going to fuck this up. I had to stop her, and the only way I knew how was to fuck her myself. Brilliant plan, Maverick. Fucking brilliant, at least my dick thinks so anyway.

She makes it difficult to focus on any task. My mind is constantly remembering how she smells, how her soft, perfect skin is like none I've ever felt before, and that fucking attitude. It should piss me off, but fuck if it doesn't excite me knowing she's a challenge. The second she told me to 'Fuck off', I wanted to remind her who she's talking to. My call name isn't Fire for nothing. Out here, she will obey me.

The kicker is, she isn't someone who submits to others. She may take my orders out here, but I know damn well she won't take them back home. No way. She's used to having control as much as I am.

I'm not into the dom/sub relationship right down to the letter, but control may as well be my middle name. I'm always in control of everything I do. The best thing for me to do for the next few days until we sneak in and make our attack is to stay the hell away from Captain Elliott.

The sound of someone entering pulls me from my thoughts. "Sir, your team is ready for tonight's training." I sit and think as Major Roberts enters my space, leaning up casually against the wall. I smile at the thought of how much torture I could put my team through during tonight's drills, but settle in knowing I can't possibly torture them any more than she will me as I fight to stay away from her.

"And we just received word that our mission will be tomorrow night. The specifics will come before nightfall." That's not much time. I wanted a few more days with the team before we throw ourselves into the mass insanity. I wanted a few more days with her to have the chance to show her I'm more than a fuck monster. Guess I'll have to make do with the time I have, which means there's no damn way that I'll be able to keep my dick in my pants, knowing our time is limited.

JADE

We've been out here for hours, going over maps of the compound we'll be attacking. Training was a breeze. Hell, I could've led that training myself. It's what we know. It's what we do.

"It's imperative that we all know every single inch of the area before we're dropped. We'll be going in late at night, surprising the motherfucker. The difficult task will be getting to TajUdin." I listen intently. Not one ounce of me is worried or scared. I'm trained to kill. I place my scope on the target and kill without any hesitation. This time will be no different.

"He'll scatter like a fucking cockroach as soon as he hears us. We'll have to flip the place upside down to find him. We'll go in dark with night vision on so this will help. I've had heat sensors added to our masks, so we should be able to see anything that has a beating heart. I have the equipment here, and we'll be adjusting everything tomorrow morning bright and early." Adrenaline begins to flow through my body. I want this guy. I hope he runs out and I get the pleasure of placing the bullet between his eyes.

"We take out everyone in the compound. No exceptions. So be prepared to kill on sight. He uses this compound as a hiding place, and we've been watching his actions for a few weeks." I continue to listen as Kaleb is in his element. He's passionate about this mission, and I can't help but follow him as he describes every aspect in full detail. The rest of my team is extremely prepared for this. I have all the confidence in the world going into this with the group of men that was chosen to walk alongside me.

"Any questions?" No one says anything, he's covered everything. He's meticulous in his detail, like he's lived this exact scenario his entire life. He's done his homework and with that, I can't help but feel completely confident and proud to be a part of this mission.

"Alright then, I need JJ and Captain Elliott to stay behind. Everyone else is free to sleep like fucking babies before all hell breaks loose tomorrow." JJ looks at me with curiosity and concern. I've been forced to stay after every single team briefing we've had, so I'm not the least bit worried about what he'll throw my way. My only concern is how I'll respond to it if he tries to consume me yet again.

"I want you here, JJ, and Elliott... you'll take the back. Stand right here once we drop you on the roof." He points to the rooftop of the large house inside the compound.

"We'll drop ropes before we land and you'll have to move fast. Our element of surprise is what will give us the advantage. If I'm waiting on you to get your asses off that rope so I can drop the rest of us, it will change the outcome of this mission. Every second counts. Can you handle this?" He looks at JJ first, then at me. Without hesitation, we both accept our assignment. Going into this with a man watching my back on that roof is exactly what we need to do.

"Thank you, JJ. You're dismissed." He didn't dismiss me. I stand with strength and will myself to be stronger than I have the past two times we've met like this. Knowing this will most likely be my last encounter with him alone, I wait for him to lead the direction this is going to go.

"Tomorrow will be intense."

"Yes, it will, Sir."

"It's an important mission and we can't fuck this up."

"I have no intentions of fucking anything up, Sir." He walks closer to me, putting his intensity into my personal space, making me feel him again. He's so fucking powerful that he radiates dominance just standing near me.

"You're going to spend the night with me." Excuse me? Has he lost his mind? There is no way in hell I'm taking a chance of getting caught. And I most assuredly do not need any more distractions. This man has already squirmed his way under my skin by taking complete control of my existence out here. He will not consume me like this. Not before this mission.

"No, I'm not."

"Do you have somewhere else you'd rather stay?"

"I didn't say that."

"Then why not?"

"Because I want to stay focused and prepare for the mission."

"That's exactly what you shouldn't do. If you worry about it, you'll start second-guessing everything. There's no way to plan for a mission like this overnight. This is what you've trained for years to do." He has a point, but I'm not staying the night with him. He needs to know that I'm not at his fucking beck and call.

He moves closer and begins to touch me, not acknowledging the 'no' that leaves as a whisper from my mouth.

My body betrays me like it does every time I'm around him. It has to stop, and yet my skin comes alive again with his touch and my heart begins to beat rapidly with anticipation of his next move. I know he'll undo me. He'll have me begging in seconds if he continues. Knowing I have no choice, I turn and begin to walk away from him. My entire body is screaming at my stupid mind that has decided to regain logic and deny him what he wants. What I want, which is everything I should stay away from. How can one man be so condescending and make me crave him all at once? He's so sure of himself.

Its dark out, the only light is the moon shining on everything, lighting it all up enough to see him when I turn around. He's following me back to my tent. I know him well enough to know he'll come right in. He doesn't have boundaries, he's proven that time and again.

I make a detour and walk him back to the structure he stays in. Turning to face him once I get there, I watch his face as he gets closer. It's almost primal. He's angry that I walked away, but I can't help him with his issues.

"Good night, Commander." I say it with finality. With every intention that those are my final words to him, but he acts like he doesn't even hear me.

His steps get faster as he nears me, with him not stopping until he's crashed into me. His hands are on my face, pulling my lips toward his in an urgency I've never felt before. I don't pull back. Hell, I don't have time to process that I need to. He invades me.

His arms move around my body, pulling me closer to him. He wraps me up in his arms and walks us both until we're inside the walls of headquarters.

My hands finally move to his back, and I slide my fingers over the ripples of muscle. He's fierce in his kiss, and I kiss him back just as hard. We explore each other's mouths with a magnitude so forceful I feel my body begin to melt, blending with the desert heat. We're ferocious, our mouths parted and tongues tangling. For the love of god, this man can kiss as well as he can fuck. He's a master at everything.

What the fuck is it about this man that makes me forget everything I've planned? It's like it is all rushed out of my head the second he causes chaos with his unpredictable intensity. How can I plan my reactions towards him when I have no idea what to expect from him at any moment?

He pulls my hair out of the tight elastic containing it, pulling me from his lips when he does. We breathe heavily together, while his eyes move across my lips before looking into my eyes.

"Don't fucking walk away from me." His voice is deep, moving straight through my body and into my core as he continues. "You waste my fucking time and yours walking away from what will goddamn happen."

He sits me on what feels like a stack of wooden boxes and quickly moves to pull off my shirt. Exposing my breasts with both hands, he moves close, licking and biting in the most perfect way. I'm not fighting him off. He feels too fucking good for that. He knows how to handle me, and I've never had someone treat me like this before. It may be fucked up, but it turns me on to a level so far beyond any man before him. There's something about knowing you're actually with a man that would be a challenge to you in a battle. Battling for control and the need to outdo each other would become a vital focus. A woman needs a man just like a strong man needs a woman. Kaleb and I could go at each other all damn day. The truth is, I've lost against him every single time. He's slowly breaking my walls down and for the life of me, I can't understand how he manages to do it every time.

He pushes me until I'm lying flat on my back, my legs still dangling off the side. His hands move fast to remove my boots and pants just before he spreads my legs and moves in.

His tongue is tight as he swirls it around, making me feel him all the way to the center of my body. He grabs my ass and lifts me closer to his face, making it almost impossible for me to stay quiet as his beard scrapes across my upper thigh. His nibble on my clit is my breaking point.

I try to squirm out of his hands, but he relentlessly holds me in place, devouring my orgasm in its entirety. His beard gives an added friction, and I find myself grinding my hips into his face before it's over. *Shit.* He's overpowering and his intensity begins to eat me alive.

I'm sensitive to his touch as I come down from the full body spasm he causes.

"See what you fucking walked away from." He unzips his pants and enters me quickly, filling me completely on the first thrust. My pussy is still throbbing, and I can feel every inch of him as he moves in and out of me. His thrusts are quick and firm, but not consistent. He's pausing between each thrust, making me think and messing with my mind.

"Look at you. You want to control this. You want me to go faster." He thrusts harder and faster, then stops just when I start to feel good again.

"Or slower." He keeps a steady pace, allowing me to get worked up before he goes back to the inconsistent thrusts.

"You can't stand the fact that I have you in a position of no control." I think about what he's saying. He's right to a point, but he needs to realize that I can still manage. Let's see how he likes this.

I slide my hand over my clit and begin to make circular movements, throwing myself forward toward another orgasm and not caring what he does. His dick is doing its job, fulfilling the need I have to feel the fullness. The rest can be done easily on my part. But I know firsthand his long, strong fingers feel better than my own.

He grabs my wrists with both hands, puts them into one grip, then reaches for the belt on the pants at his knees. I'm panting and anger surges through me. I hate that I can't scream at him and tell him exactly how I feel. *Hell, do I even know how I feel?*

He doesn't give me time to address my emotional turmoil. The thrill of his orders rings loud and clear in the deepness and in the way he speaks.

"Stand up."

I slide off the boxes, and he wraps my wrists together behind my back. He pushes my head down until I'm bent facedown against the box, then slides back into me, thrusting hard. How I'm staying quiet is beyond me. The way he glides in and out of me, hitting every nerve, makes me want to yell for more and beg to be fucked harder.

My legs and breasts feel the wood with each slam, and it isn't until he grabs my shoulder with one arm and my hair with the other that I notice what I'm lying on. The light from the moon hits it just right, so I can see what I'm smashed up against.

"What the fuck? These are explosives, Kaleb," I say quietly, knowing my eyes are wide.

"I know. How does it feel to be so fucking hot that I'd slam my dick into you on a case of explosives?" His words are powerful, but this shit scares the hell out of me. My insides freeze. Any chance of orgasm flows from my body, leaving me terrified. He slows his movements like he feels my change.

"We can do this one of two ways. You can agree to stay the night with me, or we can continue fucking right here."

He pulls his cock out and moves it to my ass, rubbing the tip over the entrance. My body defies me, and I actually spread my legs a little wider, giving him the go-ahead. The mission is tomorrow, and I know this is the last time I'll ever be with this man. I should be the one demanding everything. I'd give everything to really be able to examine his glorious cock and watch him lose control for once under my command.

I may be weak in this moment, allowing him to fuck me like this, but I'm not spending the damn night with him. No way. He continues to prime my ass with the slickness of his cock and the moisture from my pussy. I close my eyes, feeling his fingers glide between my legs, sweeping upward and stretching my ass cheeks when he slides a finger inside. My eyes snap open when the tip of his cock pushes in slowly. His dick is still wet from fucking me, and that helps him slide into my entrance.

My pussy is aching for him to return, but the more he pushes himself in, the more I feel an incredible orgasm resurface. I forget about the explosives and focus on how he makes me feel. I begin to burn with the progress he makes, slowly filling me each time. It takes a few jerky movements from his hips and complete stillness from my ass before he gets in enough to actually start moving. I feel exquisitely full. *Oh god.* Why do we have to be here? I want to yell at him to fuck me hard because right now, I need to come.

I swear he reads my mind. His movements hit rapidly. He maintains consistency when he thrusts harder, making me crazy. My skin explodes with an indescribable sensation, and I fall quickly onto the edge of an orgasm. This is my first time for this. I've never allowed another man near my ass, but god, does this feel like hell moving straight through heaven.

"Tell me I'm the first." He thrusts forward slowly, drawing my eyes back to the box below me. This speed I can handle. No sudden movements and we'll be fine, but fuck if it isn't insane trying to do this on explosives.

"Yes." I close my eyes and take the burn he's causing over every single inch of my body.

"Yes, what?" He speaks to me in a deep growl as he practically begs for my response. I know what he wants to hear.

"Yes, Sir."

CHAPTER FIVE
KALEB

She's fucking sexy as fuck. How will I let her go once this mission is over? She's perfect for me. I love the challenge of showing her she likes to submit to me and me alone.

She'd be the perfect one to show my true desires to. I can show her so much pleasure through my touch and make her feel what she's never felt before. Jade would never submit to me though. Not how I want her to. She'll test me. Piss me off and have me slapping this beautiful sweet ass that's staring me right in the face. I'd give up on trying to derive a plan to have her on her knees at my command if she agreed to take this further with me once we leave here.

I'll have to make sure this isn't the last time I'm with her. Things will be so much different when we're out of this fucking desert and home where we can learn more about each other. I want to have her in my bed, so I can show her how good I can make her feel and worship this sinful body that tempts every man who looks at her. God, I want her.

She's moaning as I fuck her slowly in the ass. It's tight, so tight that I'm only about halfway in. I love that I'm her first in this.

I drive forward a few more times before I feel her orgasm. The change causes me to dive right into my own release. She's so tiny, and I love that I can just pick her ass up and fuck her anywhere. It's a convenience that won't be lost on me if ever given the chance back in the States.

I let my eyes explore her beautiful back and ass. "Why is your back scratched all to hell?"

I step back and watch as she carefully stands away from the boxes, her eyes watching them like they're a ticking time bomb.

"Are you fucking crazy?"

"This wasn't me. If you remember, I wanted to fuck you in my cot while you stayed the night with me."

"I'm not staying with you, Kaleb."

"You will one day, and what the fuck happened to your back?" And goddamn it. She's stubborn as fuck. She will stay with me. I will make damn sure of it.

"You're so sure of yourself." I don't respond, but I am. I always get what I want, because I'm not afraid to put in the work to get it. "You happened to my back."

I try to comprehend what she's saying as she continues. "You fucked me up against that wall." It finally registers, and I begin to feel guilty for the markings all over her shoulders.

"Shit. I'm sorry."

"Don't be."

"So you liked it?" The thought of her enjoying something like that pulls my mind to a very dirty place. A place I'd love to explore with her.

I button my pants and hand her top to her, watching her as she tries to fix everything I just messed up. She has no idea how sexy this fucked look is on her.

"I'll see you tomorrow," she dismisses me before she walks out of the small shit hole I'm staying in. She fucking dismisses me. I question my damn sanity, allowing her to walk away from *me*. Tucking my head to my chin, I let out a laugh. I'm out of my fucking mind if I think she's going to break easily. Fuck. It's the other way around. She's going to be the one to break me.

I lift my head, wishing she would walk back in and stay here, letting me hold her all night. I may like control and rough, raw, gritty sex, but I'm not an asshole when it comes to the wants of a woman. Especially one like her. Her exterior shows complete hardness, but I know inside she's vulnerable. She has to hide that though; hell, we all do when we enter a place like this.

This is no place for the weak, and she sure as fuck is strong. But my beautiful Jade is soft, I can see it in her eyes and in the way she looks at me. She needs me to hold her and to tell her things that only a man would tell a woman he cares about. I'll tell her, it's breaking down those heavy walls she has up about me that will be the hard part.

She thinks all I want is to fuck her. She couldn't be more wrong. I'm way ahead of her in the caring department. I've never wanted to have a woman so bad in my life. Not until I laid my eyes on her, and I sure as fuck never wanted a woman to own me like she quickly has. When we're out of here and back on the soil of the free, I plan to show her that's exactly what we can be.

We can be free. Free to explore whatever is happening between us. Because, whether Captain Jade Elliott will admit it or not, there is definitely more to us than just sex.

"Good morning, Sir." Major Roberts walks into my office.

"Morning, Major." I gesture with my hand for him to take a seat in one of the chairs opposite of me.

"The chopper will be here at 02:00, Sir. They want us in and out and back by 06:00." *Son of a bitch.* I move quickly from my chair and grab the papers out of his hand. Scanning them over at first, I see everything seems to be in order. Then I take the time to read every word carefully. "This is it. Let's go through one more briefing with the team and make sure everyone is on the same page here." Roberts stands, spins on his boots to leave, and I sink back onto my desk when he's out of sight.

The adrenaline starts pumping through my veins. The anticipation of killing this fucker who thinks he can take out innocent women and children in his own damn country fuels me. Killing American soldiers and retaliating against our Army. I'm here to kill and to honor my fellow Americans. To first and foremost protect my country. My team and I will succeed in this mission, and the world will be a much safer place because of it.

"Motherfucker." I take off my sweat-soaked shirt, tossing the bitch in the corner of my office. Training was easy. Everyone knows what their responsibility is, right down to the two-man medical team. Aim and shoot anyone who stands in our way of killing the man we came here to kill.

What's really got my ass riled up is her. Jade. She wouldn't look at me all goddamn day. Nothing, not even when I addressed each one of them individually, making them all repeat what is expected of them and for two of them to stay together at all times.

I stared her down when I spoke to her. Telling her if she has the shot if we draw him out, she better fucking take it. She addressed me appropriately in front of her teammates with her answer, but fuck me. I need to see her up close when she talks to me. I need to taste her lips on mine one more time before we go. "Fuck." I grab a clean shirt, pulling it over my head as I walk out the door.

"Sir." I exhale, acknowledging both men on my medical team with a nod. They, too, are trained to kill.

I hold back my anger as I continue walking the small compound, looking for her. My eyes scan everywhere, from the tiny tent we eat under to hers. Where in the hell is she?

The sun is setting deep in the desert. Soon we'll be going from closing out one day and right into the next. The day we've prepared for. The day that will forever be engrained into our memories as one of the craziest times of our lives. When our lives were in danger and we were on a mission to kill anything that moves.

I finally see her. She's standing off to the side of my tent. Our eyes lock. This shit is forbidden out here. It's dangerous for me to keep my observance of her, exploiting what I desperately want to say. I know the look on my face will give away the desperation I'm feeling inside.

She drags her gaze away first and tucks her blond hair under her hat, disregarding me as if I never existed. I watch closely as she makes her way to JJ, tucking herself close to his side. I lose sight of her when they enter the equipment area... The one that I fucked her in last night.

It kills me more than I care to admit that he's the one with her right now instead of me. He'll be with her on top of that roof, guarding her back the same way she'll be guarding his. He's a good man and a dedicated soldier, not only to this country, but to his wife and children as well. "Take care of her JJ, I need her," I whisper to myself.

"You worried about her?" Roberts comes up behind me. I scoff at the absurdity of his question. That woman has more balls than most men I've met.

"Not at all. She's more put together than the rest of us. She can handle this." Speaking the damn truth, I know Jade can handle it. It's my damn feelings for her that need to be handled before I fuck this shit all up. A mind must be clear during a mission. A single hesitation could cost a life, so I need to get my shit in check quickly.

I need to focus on being an expert, as well as the leader of this team for the next few hours, while we compile our gear. Then tear down what we can to help the cleaners who will come in the minute we leave and demolish this small camp like it never existed. All teams leave out today. Not a damn thing will be left behind, only memories.

Memories should be left behind here in this mass destruction, this place called hell. Mine will exist.

With determination, I enter my office to send one last email to Colonel Wright, who I will report back to the minute we land in the United States.

Closing my laptop, I tuck it safely into my duffle bag that will await me at the airport in Dubai. I stand, roam to my small cot, and sit on the edge to set my alarm on my watch, knowing damn well I won't sleep. Not out of fear for our mission. I'm fearful of her and of what the fuck will become of us after we're all debriefed and go our separate ways.

Will she act as if I never existed, the same way she did the entire night we tore shit down? Or will she want to exist in my world and get to know me? Will she want me the same way I want her? What she fails to know about me is, I'm not a man to give up on the things I want; and I want her. Not just her body, but her soul and her heart.

As I lay my head on my pillow, I close my eyes. I don't sleep. I'm ready for this mission. I'm focused. I have to be. I have men to protect. A woman to protect. "I will own you, Jade. You will become mine." Those are the last words I speak before I succumb to the sleep I didn't think I would get.

The distinctive sound of the MH-60 Black Hawk Helicopter approaching rings in our ears. Everyone is geared up and dressed in darkness with our backpacks attached. Each one of us carries several rifles and pistol mags, a radio, and hydration reservoirs. Watching everyone with special ops helmets in hand, I stand secure, knowing they're designed to stop a round from a pistol busting open a skull. These helmets are lightweight but carry the necessities needed to guide us through the dark. Flashlights, cameras, ear and microphone pieces all in place and tested repeatedly. All exposed skin painted, making us inconspicuous to the enemy. We are fucking ready.

No one speaks as we watch the helicopter land; instead we're running toward it. The high-pitched whirl of the engine and the blades strum over the loud beating of our pounding chests.

"Let's do this. In and out. I don't give two fucks who kills that bastard as long as the proof is recorded. I also don't give a shit who you take down to get to him. Do I make myself clear?" I yell over the top of the roaring engines as we lift off of the ground. My eyes are trained on Jade, who looks straight ahead, still not meeting my eyes. I need to drive my point deep into them all.

My meaning is really meant for her more than anyone else. I've kept this to myself until now, but I saw the way she looked at the women and children during our briefing a few days ago. She stayed tight-lipped, like she should. But her eyes gave her away, showing a flicker of sadness. Grief before we even strike. It's a sore spot with most soldiers. It's one thing to kill the enemy, but when the enemy is a child or a woman, it's a hard pill to swallow.

Every facet of flying at night is unlike flying in the clear gleam of the day. Pitch black awaits you; the only lights you see are the red panels lit up from the cockpit, illuminating the determination of the pilot. Silence awaits. Blood begins to boil in anticipation, and I start to remember why I craved this kind of shit for so long in my career.

Then before I know it, the smallest of light appears on the ground and the one person I care about drops into place beside me. I close my eyes for a brief second and take in her close proximity. I'd love more than anything to take her in my fucking arms and tell her the shit that's boiling up inside me. 'Be fucking careful, Jade. Know your strengths and acknowledge your weaknesses. It makes you invincible when you work with the knowledge of both. Don't let your guard down, and for fuck's sake, don't hesitate. Do what you've been trained to do.'

"Captain," I whisper. Her head jerks my way. I can no longer see her stunning eyes. I reach for her hand, grasp it firmly in mine. That's all I can give her, all she lets me have as we glide in closer to the building.

The thick woolen ropes are attached to the cabin drop. Right behind them, JJ and Jade fast-rope down and just like that, she's gone. She's out of sight, but not even close to being out of mind.

I nod to the pilot and we lift several feet; then in one giant swoop, we drop. It's fast and quick, just like we planned. Everyone jumps out and scatters into their positions. We're behind enemy territory. We've just jumped without hesitation straight into what we all know will be a bloodbath before this is over. Just as quickly as he dropped us off, the pilot is gone, waiting in the darkness to return.

"I need a status from my snipers." Whispering is hard when your heart is racing from the adrenaline of a run like this, but it helps when I get the go-ahead from both Jade and JJ. Knowing she's in position and safe makes me feel like I can go in and kill this motherfucker.

Lights start to turn on in several of the buildings. Harris, Roberts, and I move toward the building where we know Azham-Amir-TajUdin is hiding.

"Fuck. Everyone down," I say into my microphone when several men run into the dingy street. Flashlights, guns, and grenades in hand, I look to Harris for his interpretation when they start yelling in their native tongue.

"Someone's here. Someone's here. Attack. Attack," he whispers.

The second we hunch down to the ground, all hell breaks loose. Gunshots start to go off into the air, and I watch as three of the men in the street are taken out with one single gunshot to the head before the rest retreat back into the darkened shadows, shooting at JJ and Jade as they go. I know they've missed my team, because I can hear moving through my earpiece.

We move. I have no fear. I lead us into the building and know without a doubt they have that fucker buried in here to keep him safe. He's no leader. He's a damn pussy motherfucker, who gives orders to kill, to rape, and to mutilate, while he sits here in his fucking hideout, letting these suicide assholes do all his work. A true leader doesn't expect his teammates to do anything he wouldn't do. These men and women have been brainwashed for years. It's like one giant piece of rotting shit that's broken off and fed to the next person in line. They're born to live a life not worth living. It's so wrong. They make themselves our enemy and we make them dead as fuck.

I have no control of what's happening outside of this building. I'll have to leave that up to my team. Gunshots ring in my ears while my men talk to each other, having our backs the farther we creep into the building.

We make a dirty sweep of the main floor of the distraught building, killing over a dozen men. Fuck, call me sick and twisted, but this is the shit I live for. To kill. It's unfortunate for every one of these fuckers who is now bleeding to death, trying to scatter away like fucking cockroaches crawling along the dirty floor. Or a snake slithering away after you've cut off its head. Pathetic fucking creatures. It's time these assholes die.

They're the enemy because they, too, crave the kill. Ours. There is no fucking way I'm accepting that as our fate as I continue to leave a path of bodies behind me as I search for this fucker. I move up to one filthy asshole, his tongue dragging out of his mouth as he screams what I assume is obscenities directly in my face. "Fuck you." I pull out my .45 and shoot him right between his eyes.

You don't have time to blink in this situation. We are moving fast as we sweep further into the building. "Bingo, bitches." I smile and signal for Roberts to toss a grenade.

Jade's face flashes across my mind for one brief moment. I know she's alright. They all are. I would know. It's only been a few minutes since we began this battle. Very little communication is needed, but I have my ears tuned into her. I know she's breathing in my ear. It may have something to do with the fact that she's the only one in my left ear. Call me controlling, I don't give a fuck. I knew her safety would keep me clear-headed.

Her face drops out of my memory as quickly as it invades it. I nod for the go-ahead the second the three of us have retreated back down the hallway we just came through. The sound of the pin being pulled and the launching of the tiny yet powerful vessel being sent into the air takes me back in time. The sweet sound of the clapping thunder from the explosion when it hits its target has my cock twitching, and I fucking love the rush that consumes me.

We move fast through the cloud of smoke, heading toward the light shining from a room on the left. Screaming women, who I don't trust one damn bit, submerge from their huddles. Harris stands over them with two pistols in his hands, while Roberts and I battle it out with three guards who barrel at us with a knife in one hand and guns in the other. Fucking war. I take one out while he takes out another. The last one is quick, his shot barely missing Roberts.

"Time to die, motherfucker." I snap his hand behind his back until I hear it crack, allowing the gun to fall to the floor.

"Ask him where he is, Harris." I spin the fucker around, and Harris mumbles some bullshit jargon. The soldier dressed all in black spits in his direction. I shove him forward and put a bullet straight through the back of his head.

"Roberts. Where the fuck—" I turn around to face our enemy, my words cut off mid-sentence. The one whose life I'm about to take is standing before me. Roberts has the fucker's hands behind his back, his once white cloak now stained and dirty just like his heart.

"You Americans cannot come in here and do this. This is wrong." He speaks in English. Of course he knows English. To hear my native tongue flowing out of his mouth has my hands itching to cut his tongue out.

"Wrong?" I question, my brows lifting. "This is right, bitch. Back away from him, Roberts." The instant Roberts moves out of the way, I send the last four rounds from my mag straight the fuck into his black soul.

"Snake down." Our code that he's dead echoes through our ears. This means the chopper is on its way back. It'll be here in three minutes tops. The women are folding their hands together, rocking back and forth in the corner, screaming. They're obviously praying for the death of this so-called leader. I release the clip on my camera and shove my evidence deep inside my pocket.

We leave the exact same way we came in, but now the silence greets us in the half-lit street. We run along the sides of the buildings, never cowering, yet always keeping cover.

I list off every member of my team into my headpiece. They all answer back with their chosen code word assigned to them during training. When I hear her sweet voice answer with the word 'hunger', my lips tilt upwards. Our mission is over, and she has no idea just how hungry I am for her.

CHAPTER SIX
JADE

It's a difficult task to try to get into the mind of a sniper, and it's by far more strenuous to live as one. I've trained for this, studied usage in weapons, how to handle stressful situations and the ability to accept any challenge set in front of me, and I'm proud to say I've always succeeded in my missions.

Your mind has to be in the right place. Our emotions are demanding. Summing it up, you have to literally require your mind to not only do the work it needs to do on the inside to keep you alive, you also have to let it take over every aspect and every grueling detail on the outside.

It's JJ and I up here. Each of us trained to do this with the privilege to see through our night vision gear as if it's daylight. Our eyes have to be everywhere. My sights are zeroed in, and I'm ready to pull the trigger at any moment.

That's why I stayed as far away from Kaleb as I could today. He's a distraction out here I can't afford. Not only for myself, but for every single one of my teammates, including him. One slipup, one miss, and we could jeopardize this entire mission. Or worse yet, lose a member of the team. As hard as it is to snub out another life and watch them die unexpectedly from your hand, there is no way in hell I will lose my focus and take a chance on losing one of the guys. To have to live the rest of my life knowing it was my fault would be worse than death to me.

I felt Kaleb's eyes on me all day. The urge to run to him ran through my veins as fast as the blood coursing through them. I may be an American soldier, but I'm a woman. I have a need to be held every once in a while, and I'd love to have someone tell me they care.

I know he's not that man. God, how I wish he were. He's crawled under my skin during the past few days. Every waking moment, all I can think about is him. I'm a fool for believing him when he told me we would continue this once we arrive back home. I'm sure he's a liar, a manipulator, and I let him take me without knowing a damn thing about him. It's easy to say one thing in the sweltering heat of the desert, then change it completely once you hit safe land. The desert makes you fucking crazy.

Now, as I lie on top of this roof with my rifle in position and my finger on the trigger, ready to fire the instant I need to, I've made one decision. I hope I never see him again after this is over. My heart clenches at the thought of not having his hands on me again. He's possessed me in a way I can't describe. Deep down I know he only used me every time he fucked me. I have to be done. I have to go back to the States with a clear head and try to return to some sense of normalcy. After tonight, he no longer has control of anything I do or say. During training, there was a hole drilled so deep into our heads that once a mission is over it is never spoken of again. Everything that happens is left here. And that has to include him.

I'm thankfully pulled away from the last thoughts I will allow myself to have of Kaleb the second several men barge out of a building, screaming. JJ and I are undetected up here, and that gives us a great advantage. The moment those fuckers start shooting their guns in the air, we take them out. One right after the other, they drop to the ground. My intellect is not giving a shit that I've just snuffed out several human beings' lives. These fuckers deserve to die. Every damn one of them.

JJ nudges me, his fingers coding that he's spotted two men climbing up the roof of a building across from us. I aim my rifle, find my target, and take them both out, their shit bodies falling to the ground.

I have no idea how many more we kill. I do know the instant I see three women coming out of a darkened building, I hold off and watch them. Fuck. Sweat starts to drip down my back and forehead. "Goddamn it," I say while covering my microphone with two of my fingers.

One of them places her hand inside her dark-colored clothing. Threat or not, they have to go. JJ takes out two of them, and I hit the other. I sigh in relief. Minutes go by quickly. All we hear is the firing of guns from inside the building where we know our main target is. The beautiful moment we hear Kaleb announce it's done is the second JJ pulls out his bomb. He does his thing to set it and we're gone.

Crawling across the hard pebbles of this soon-to-be destroyed building is one of the hardest things. We have to get our asses out of here now. Our shit will blow up if we stall too long. JJ hits the steps alongside the roof first, and I follow close on his ass. Feet planted on the rusty steps, rifle slung over my back, I haul ass. We hit the ground and run for the empty field we've been instructed to meet in.

I hear his voice once again. Deep, dark, and dangerous as he asks each one of us to give our code word. I'm the last one to rattle mine off. Each of us was given a word we were to check in once the mission was complete. "Hunger," I say loudly, my breathing rapidly picking up speed the faster I run.

The helicopter approaches; one by one, everyone jumps in. Except me.

I can't explain the sudden urge of panic that catastrophically hits me in the gut. It's as if my sensors are telling me something is wrong. I turn my body sharply in the direction of the small village. Kaleb, Harris, and Roberts are still running toward us.

"Did you see that?" I yell over the top of the blaring engines of the helicopter.

"See what?" one of the guys yells back from inside the chopper.

"There's someone running behind them. Fuck!" I scream as I snatch my weapon, aim my scope, and crouch down low.

It's a damn young boy. My hands begin to shake and my eyes start to water. Everything happens so fast. I watch the young kid, who can't be over the age of twelve or thirteen, stop running.

He aims two guns in our direction. Then quickly, his arms shift and he's pointing them at Kaleb, who's the last one of the three.

"Shoot him, Elliott! Now! Damn it!" JJ roars. My mind is racing as I watch his every move.

"Please put the guns down, boy," I whisper. He doesn't. Of course he won't. These children are brainwashed to believe we are the enemy. Some are stolen from their families, only to become trained killers. Not in the way we train. No, they train to hate and even kill their own flesh and blood if told to.

With perfect hands, I shoot. The young boy flies backwards, but not before he fires off two shots. I can't think. I can barely see. My vision blurs, and I drop my weapon. My entire being is trembling as the reality of what I've done slams into my chest.

The last thing I allow my brain to remember as I stare into the hard eyes of Kaleb Maverick is the sound of the bomb. The echo of the aircraft as it lifts and shoots round after round from the attached machine guns and the fact that not only have I killed a child, but I've been shot.

CHAPTER SEVEN
JADE

"Sir, you can't be back here." My restless mind is desperately trying to decipher the female voice. I'm groggy, light-headed, and confused. I blink rapidly, fighting the blinding light as I try to open my eyes and focus.

"Elliott." I try to sit up at the mention of my name, only to have soft but firm hands hold me still. "Captain, please stay still." I turn in the direction of the female voice.

"Where am I?" I question, my mouth dry. Jesus, my head hurts. Pain shoots through my forearm when I try to lift it to my aching head. White gauze is wrapped around my arm, the tightness constricting me from moving it up or down to inspect what the hell is happening.

"To answer your question, Captain, you're at Landstuhl Regional Medical Center in Germany." I look down to her name tag that reads Dr. Vivian Brooks.

"How the hell did I get here?"

"You were injured. Are you capable of telling me what you remember?" My head whips around to the other side of the bed where I lie stiff and sore when a deep voice clears his throat.

"Kaleb." My eyes speak for themselves. They look him up and down. It's the first time I've seen him dressed this casually. His dark jeans and white t-shirt stretch tight across his manly chest. I may be somewhat disoriented, but my god, he is just so damn beautiful. His blue eyes are vibrant and his arms more defined than I remember. His tattoos have my mouth watering when seconds ago it was dry and his piercings are blatantly obvious in his shirt.

"Hey," he speaks quietly.

"Hey," I say back, then turn my eyes away from him. He shouldn't be here. I remember everything; all of it. Every fuck, every thrust, every kiss.

I jerk my hand away from him when he reaches for it. He retreats his without a word. I focus my attention on the doctor. "I was shot," is all I say. It's all I can say, all I'm aloud to say.

Her mouth smiles kindly. "You were grazed by the bullet. It did not hit you. You have five stitches, and you will be in pain for a few days, Captain."

"Oh. Well, that's great," I manage to say rather weakly. I have so many questions to ask. Like how in the hell I flew six and a half hours from Afghanistan to Germany without remembering a damn thing.

"You'll be free to fly back to the States tomorrow morning. Tonight, I want you to rest." She looks from me to Kaleb as if her statement was meant for him.

"I'm not leaving, Doc. No fucking way," he states demandingly.

"He's fine." I have things I want to talk to him about. He's one of the only people who can answer all of my questions.

"Very well. I'll be back to check on you. If you need anything at all, please push this button and a nurse will help you with anything you need." She pats my leg lightly. I watch her back until she disappears.

For the first time since I laid my eyes on Kaleb Maverick, I'm alone with him, free to do whatever I want with him, yet wanting absolutely nothing to do with him.

"Why are you here?" I can't help but sound irritated.

"Where the fuck else would I be?" He sits back in his chair, kicked back, allowing my eyes to fall to his chest rising as he waits for my response.

"I don't know, but I don't need your ass watching over me. I'm fine."

"I never said you did. I'm here for me." Does he really think I'm an idiot?

"What exactly does me getting shot have to do with you?"

"You saved my ass in that mission." He sits up, leaning closer to the bed. Closer to me. Bringing his intensity into my bubble yet again.

"You're welcome." My sarcasm escapes before the nightmare flashes through my mind. I can see the boy's face. He was on a mission to kill him, just like we were on a similar mission to kill anything in our way. He was so young, and it guts me to think of the shit these people feed their children just to attempt to get a surprise shot in on the enemy. Do they not have boundaries in their country to protect their futures and the people who will one day be the generation making decisions for them?

Tears fill my eyes as I replay the memories of watching him fall to the ground. I killed a child. I aimed my rifle at him and took the shot, knowing I would not miss. Flames fill my mind, pull me back to my conversation with Kaleb.

"Where's everyone else? Tell me they all made it out. Harris?" He stands when I ask about Harris. A ping of jealousy rushes across his face, but I don't care. I don't have time for his bullshit games. Harris is and will always be a soldier I care about.

"He's fine. He just left to get something to eat down the hall."

"He's here too?" The surprise in my voice is obvious. Since when did I become the bitch who needs bedside monitoring? I attempt to wipe the tears from my face and change the subject from what's truly burning me from the inside out.

"Yes. He disregarded my orders to leave. We need to talk about that."

"What's there to talk about?" Harris is a grown man who can make his own decisions. The mission is over. He has no say what any of us can do. Not anymore.

Kaleb stands over me. His eyes search for mine, and I quickly look down at my hands against the white sheet over my legs. I move the fingers of my good arm over the material and try to ignore the heat he's sending into my core. He makes me feel nervous as he stands there, and I welcome the sound of the door as Harris walks back in.

"Good fucking morning, Elliot. It's nice of you to join us."

"Fuck off, Harris. Should've known you'd be eating while some of us here are having to do all the work." I'm not finished talking before he sits on the opposite edge of the bed from Kaleb and wraps his arms over my shoulders, being gentle as he does so.

"Leave it up to you to try to get a fucking nap in on the job." I smile as he continues to tease me while Kaleb stays quiet. He remains standing and doesn't move an inch from his very close position right next to the bed.

My eyes graze his, and I try to think of the best way to get him to leave. Harris may need to be my out on this.

"Everyone else okay?" Looking at Harris, I begin to ignore Kaleb. Or at least it appears that way. My body knows he's here, and no matter how hard I try to disregard him, I can't. He's under my skin and that makes a very bad recipe for disaster as I'm preparing to spend some time at home.

"All good. A few were banged up a bit there at the end, but nothing a little rest can't handle. It seems they're all excited to get the orders to head home to the States."

"That sounds amazing." It's been two years since I've seen most of my family in person. I know they miss me, and in a way I'm ready to be home, but I've left a piece of me behind in that desert. A piece I'm hoping like hell I'll be able to cope with losing.

I continue to keep my issues hidden from the guys. I'm dying inside. I want to cry and scream from the top of my lungs for what I've done, but given the situation again, I'd do the same damn thing. I'd have to. He was aiming directly at my Commander. My job is to protect my team, no matter who I have to take out to do that.

I force myself to set it all to the back of my mind. There's plenty of time for me to deal with that in the days to come.

"You headed back home to Florida?" Harris' hand on my leg pulls me from my thoughts. I'm due to have six months leave until I'm scheduled to return, but honestly, I don't know how long I have. I've signed up to return at any given point I'm needed. It's why I pushed myself so hard all these years to be the best I can be. I'm in the elite group of snipers they call on, and I'm willing to do what it takes to remain there.

"For a little while anyway. I may try to find some place secluded and take some vacation time." The thought of seeing my family trying to strap down my thoughts has me very much wanting to ask for a phone, to hear their voice.

Kaleb moves to sit down. I ignore the pull that I feel when he transfers his sexy body into the chair. He was a great fuck. He was an outstanding leader, who assembled the perfect team to successfully pull off this mission, but that's where he ends with me. His barbaric ways of trying to control me have to come to a stop.

The door opens again, and I see JJ's concerned face relax as he sees me. "I'm finally cleared." The guys act like we've been here for days. The very thought of that has me curious as to just exactly how long I was out for.

"How long have we been here?"

"It's been twenty-four hours." Harris surprises me with his response. How in the hell was I out that long?

JJ moves in closer and bumps my fist in a greeting. They've shifted forward and stare at me as they both talk. Harris begins to smile at me, and I wait for his teasing to begin once again.

"Don't mind Elliot, she's been fuckin sleeping for days."

"Yeah, well, she scared the shit out of me out there." JJ stands at the foot of my bed and glances toward Kaleb.

"I'm fine. Just a graze." These guys will annoy the crap out of me if they keep this shit up.

"It's that precise shooting of yours that saved a few of them from having a bullet up their asses." He's right. I look down at the sheets as they continue to talk about it in a general way, never giving a single detail of where we've been or what we've done. There aren't any ears in this room that weren't there, but the orders were to be silent once we're done, so that's what I'll do.

I'll return to my hometown and just like always, I won't tell a single soul that I've killed many men and even a few women in my time away; but this time I'll also be keeping the death of a child deep inside. I've been through sensitivity training to prepare me for the psychological burdens of shit like this, but the hell burning in me right now as I try to pretend to be completely fine is taking over.

I lay my head back on the pillow and use my good arm to hold my aching forehead. "Can I get some rest, guys? My head is killing me." I shouldn't need the rest. It's more of the fact that I just want to be alone. I need to think.

Both Harris and JJ nod at me before they assure me they'll be here until I get the clear to leave. I'm the last one, so I'll need to get my shit together if I'm ever going to want some peace and quiet. They'll go stir crazy and make me insane if I'm here for too long.

Kaleb doesn't move. He has no intention of leaving, and I begin to wonder how exactly I'm going to handle that. He's fucking stubborn. I've only known him for a few days, but the one thing I know about him is, he doesn't give in. When he wants something, he gets it, and fuck any of the consequences.

"Can you let me rest?" I try to get him to leave and get the weight of his stare off my chest, but of course he doesn't budge.

"Yes, please rest." He's still not moving.

"I think you should leave." I work myself up to let those words escape. I want to cry and have a motherfucking moment where I can actually deal with what I've done, and he's being difficult.

"I'm not leaving you, Jade." He moves his chair closer and grabs my hand. I both hate it and love it. I want to be alone, but

I want to be with someone who understands the shit I've done. I can't think with him this close, and the chaos is taking over my head.

"Please, just let me be alone." I can't hold back the tears any longer. "Please, Kaleb. Please go." I roll to the shoulder opposite of him and let the tears run into the pillow. I feel him moving away before I hear the latch on the door. His footsteps return just before he slides behind me on the bed.

He wraps his giant arm over mine and pulls me into his body. His face settles against my cheek, and I listen as he speaks to me.

"Jade. I'm not leaving you, because I know you're hurting. You saved my fucking life out there, and I know it's eating you alive. You can't talk about it, so you won't, but I refuse to let it kill the beautiful Jade inside I'm fucking dying to get to know in person. I'm staying with you. I'm going home with you, and I'm fucking making you stay the goddamned night with me because you owe me a night even though I owe you for saving my life. You will not let this eat you alive. You will accept the brutality of this nightmare as doing what you had to do to save your team, and you will move forward from this mission to do great shit. I know you will, because I'm never wrong." His arm tightens and the weight of his face against my cheek becomes heavier as he relaxes against me. The tears don't stop falling, and I let him hold me, because frankly, it feels good being in his arms when I'm hurting. I feel like in this moment, I'm safe from all the nightmares and danger this fucked-up job causes.

KALEB

I can't stand knowing I've let this happen to her. I should've seen the kid. I should've pulled the fucking trigger and spared her from this, but I didn't. I know she'll come back from being this trigger-shy when it comes to the same scenario. I've seen it before. Soldiers often lock up after something like this. She needs to know she did not do this. The fucked-up nation training babies to kill did this.

I hold her against me with the only purpose of consoling her. I want her to know I'm not just after her for a great fuck, because shit if it isn't the best with her. She's beautiful, and right now she's broken. It's my job to make sure she's able to put the pieces back together.

I need to take her back to my compound in Missouri. She can work with me there to put this behind her and ensure she won't let it hinder her reaction time in the future.

Her skin is soft, but I'm not feeling that. Her ass is against my cock, but I'm not feeling that, either. She's curled into my arms for a while before I feel her relax. Her breaths slow, and I know she's asleep in my arms. This is exactly what I've been dying to feel. I love every moment she's able to be with me like this. I only wish it wasn't under her duress. The anguish she's holding in is fucking killing me.

The door rattles and the nurse begins to knock obsessively. I'm left with only one option. I have to get up and open the door. Jade doesn't turn to me, nor does she wake when I get up to open it, and she keeps her back to me once I sit back down.

"Looks like the bird will be here in the morning to move your team, Commander. It's been a pleasure treating your crew." She moves over Jade, who has woken up, her eyes sleep-deprived even though she's been out for a day. She begins checking her once again, then stands at attention, waiting for my final dismissal. We're going home. It hasn't been long for me, but it's still a great feeling coming off of a mission like that.

It's time to return to the land of the free and this time, I'm going home with someone I look forward to spending time with. One mission down, now it's time to successfully complete the mission where I make her mine. She has no idea how hard I've fallen for her. Hell, I thought I had it bad before I hit that desert, but now that I've had her in my arms and around my dick, there's no chance I won't go all in to try to make her mine. I want her to crave me and to beg for me to touch her like I do when I'm near her. I want to consume her like she does me.

She needs to live a little. There's so much more to life than she realizes. I desperately want to hear her laugh, to see her eyes light up from the simplest touch. To have her kiss me hungrily, to ravage every part of her body, not fuck her, but love her. I'm going to break her shell she has herself cocooned in and crack that fucker wide open. There's beauty inside there, and it's all mine to explore.

"I can walk, you guys. Good lord!" Jade yells, and I mean yells, at Harris and JJ when they try to help her out of the back of the car when we arrive at the airport. Jesus Christ, this is bound to be a long ass flight, especially if these assholes don't keep their hands off of her.

"Quit being a bitch," Harris snaps. I know the two of them are close, but fuck him. Calling her a bitch in front of me is taking it a bit far. Joking or not, that shit doesn't sit well with me.

"That's enough. Jade, get your ass out of the car and into the airport. Now." I point my finger toward the shiny revolving doors.

"Yes, Sir." Christ almighty, the way she says that. Her defying gaze has my cock twitching. Like I said, this is going to be a long ass flight.

She climbs out of the car, her ass plastered in the sexiest fucking pair of jeans with rhinestones on the back. My cock isn't twitching anymore. He's gone straight to trying to sniff his way out of my jeans. And that shirt, it's a plain V-neck, but holy hell, does she make it look good stretched across those perfectly crafted tits. I am so fucked.

She walks around all three of us, snatches her bag out of the trunk, and with her ass swaying takes off walking away from us. Fuck me.

"You hungry?" I sneak up behind her after we've cleared security.

"No. I could use some water, though, to take one of these pain pills." She smiles even though I know it's fake. I need to pull her off to the side and ask her what the hell her problem is, but first I need to get rid of these two.

"I'm going to grab something to eat. I'll get the water and some food for you, Jade. If you don't fucking eat it, then I'll turn you over my knee and gladly spank that tight ass. Nice jeans by the way." Harris isn't tactful with his shit way of expressing how much he wants her. He's damn sure got another thing coming if he thinks he's going to get anywhere near her ass. She walks away, glaring at me without a word. She knows damn well I'm not going to say a word. Yet anyway.

Harris lifts his brows at her in a way I don't like at all. Those two little slits he sees out of are half hanging out of his damn head, stuck right on her ass, and I pull back from attacking him right here in front of everyone... Motherfucker. He has no chance in hell against me. She won't even consider him after I'm finished with her. I feel my hands clenching into tight fists at my sides. This fucker is pushing my limits, and I'm about to knock him straight on his ass. I just need time with her by myself, in my own environment. I want to treat her like the woman I know she is and deserves to be.

"It's a long flight, I'll go with you. Commander, what would you like?" Now if Harris would be more like this polite kid and not send those fucking sexual innuendos around like he can't wait to try to get into those sexy panties I saw her shimmy into back at the hospital this morning, then I might like the dude.

"Doesn't matter. I'll eat anything. Why don't you get us all something?" I curl my lip, never taking my eyes off of Jade, while

I dig out a handful of twenties, count out four, and hand them over to him.

"I'll buy everyone's." I nod in his direction, my eyes never leaving hers. I see her, she can't fool my ass. Her breathing speeds up and her cheeks flush. Damn, she's gorgeous as she stands there trying to pretend I don't affect her.

These are the things I want to see on her. I bet anything if I dipped my hand into the front of her jeans, scraped my fingers around the edge of those silky panties, moved them down the seam, she'd be wet as fuck.

"Perfect timing, beautiful. Come here." My hand reaches out, pulling her flush against me. My back is to the wall, and she comes to me willingly. She has to, there are way too many people here to cause a scene. I'm about ready to stir her up and shake her to her damn core.

"What the hell are you doing?" She snips into my ear.

"Staking a claim right now." My mouth takes hers. She resists me at first, then fuck, her hands land on my chest. She's warm and completely intoxicating. My tongue swipes against hers the second she opens up to me, and she moans into my mouth.

Shit, the sound of her voice drives me insane. The only thing I can think of is getting her alone, with no one around us for miles, just so I can hear those sweet little sounds escaping from her mouth, so I can tell her exactly what she does to me. No restrictions. No boundaries. No rules. Just us and this fiery hot chemistry we have between us.

"Kaleb, what the hell are you doing?" She tries to pull away. Hell to the motherfucking no. She is not getting away from me.

"Don't stand there and pretend like you don't want it. You want this as much as I do." I press my engorged cock against her and she gasps.

"There are people watching us." She chooses right now to be shy. I shrug. I really don't care; let them look. I'll teach them all how this is done.

"Harris is going to get his ass beat if he says one more word to you. It would be different if his intentions were noble, but we both know they aren't. He wants you." Her gaze borders on the verge of a smug smile. She knows damn well that shit is getting to me.

"You have nothing to be jealous of. I'm not yours, nor am I his, and if you don't get that through your thick alpha skull, I won't let your ass near me. Check yourself, Maverick. I'm not a fucking piece of property for you to own, and I'm sure as fuck not a piece of meat for you two to tear apart while you fight over me." I pull her wrist against my side, while she spews her words in my face.

She's feisty and not at all afraid to tell me off and remind me how it is. Goddamn, she will be so much fun to play with when I get her back home. The thoughts of all the possibilities cause a smile on my face, which only pisses her off even further.

"Kaleb. I'm tired. I'm not dealing with this pissing match. You're going to have to get over yourself and relax a little."

"I'll relax when I can slip inside that sweet pussy of yours again. Until then, I'm going to be worked up. It comes with the territory of running a big mission like this. I'll need to blow off this aggression somehow, and I can only think of one way that sounds perfect."

"Do you always think with your dick?"

"No. I assure you, honey, there's so much more of me craving you than just my dick. I'm not just here to fuck around, Jade." I pull her closer as I speak close to her ear. She tucks her arms into my chest as I wrap my arms around her before she pushes away. Her hurt arm is wrapped, but she's still moving it.

Using her big, beautiful eyes to look straight into mine, she begins again. "You're insane. Kaleb, please don't do this shit in front of the guys anymore. I won't have anyone thinking I'm fucking my way into these missions. I've worked too damn hard for my career to throw it all away like that. I respect these guys, and I want them to continue to respect me. Just because I had a lapse in judgement a few times with you doesn't mean I'm yours to toy with for all eternity."

I open my mouth to respond to her lapse of judgment lie, a damn hit to my fucking gut, but see Harris behind her, returning with a shit ton of food in his arms. She turns to see what my eyes are focused on and instantly moves to help him. He must be telling fucking jokes when she reaches him, because she throws her head back and smiles the largest smile I've ever seen on her face. My heart skips at least once, knowing I've never been the reason for her happiness. That's something I plan to change very soon.

JJ and Roberts walk up from their trip to find the latrine, and I exhale knowing I've fucked up my last moment alone with her. From here on out, the team will be tight in our vicinity. I know my seat is next to hers, and I made sure JJ is on the opposite side of her. Harris is in a different fucking row, and I don't give two shits who he's stuck next to. The guy had my back on that mission, but I know damn well he's not on my side when it comes to Jade.

I don't eat anything he brings back, but I do watch them all interact as a group of great friends. That's what I miss most about being active. The comradery among the guys begins lifelong friendships that lead to so much support, and in the worst cases, heartache as they all come home from the extremities of being on active duty.

Lives change and evolve like the seasons, and a soldier deals with the most extreme cases of that. Going from training for years then to active duty for even more, it's extremely difficult to fit in at home after being away for so long. I should know, I still don't. I have my brothers. Brothers I met when I served and who haven't faltered since. My real blood brother is a piece of shit who doesn't even deserve a mention from my mouth. He'll get his one day. I don't even have to serve it to him. He fucks up enough that karma will do its job.

Her laughter pulls me from my thoughts, and I watch her stand to land a punch to Harris' shoulder, tucking her injured arm against her body. I wish to fuck it was a real punch to his face, but it wasn't. It was more like a playful, flirty slug that just irritates the shit out of me. I can either stand back here and sulk, or join the party.

I guess it's time I start to play the game. I don't lose. I want her, and I will make her see that we're going to be great together. She's just not in the right mindset to focus on that right now. There are too many emotions at the surface with everything that's going on for her to think about anything except going home.

They finally call our flight to begin boarding, and I stand quickly to grab my carry-on bag, picking up hers as I do. She takes it from me and throws it over her good shoulder with a quiet 'thanks' before walking to the line of people ready to board. I fall in behind them all and wait patiently for my chance to spend hours next to her.

This will be a chance to talk to her about real life. I want to know everything about her, and today is where that journey continues.

An elderly couple steps near me, and I use my hand to let them go in front of me. There's no hurry to board a plane that has assigned seats. My bag fits below the one in front of me, so I'm not in any rush.

They fumble with their boarding passes before we finally move through the doors and I cross over from solid concrete to the temporary walkway leading up to the airplane, welcoming the shift of my environment. This is another step of many with her, and I let the smile grace my face with the anticipation of what's to come.

Stepping onto the crowded airplane, I quickly see Harris leaning over Jade. I watch JJ stand and cut the line of passengers off as he crosses into the other row of seats. He sits in what should be Harris' seat, and my anger instantly boils to the surface. That motherfucker needs to be taught a damn lesson in survival. Rule number one.... Don't fuck with my woman. Rule number two... Don't fuck with me.

The smile on my face has been replaced with hatred as I watch him have her move to the window seat. He takes the middle, and I begin to plan where I'll stab this asshole first. "Fucking dick." I didn't mean to say that out loud, but from the looks I'm getting, apparently I did.

I finally arrive at my fucked-up destination, my eyes focused on Harris. My mind made up that I'll just yank the cocky asshole out of the seat next to her and sit there myself. It's as simple as that. The fight won't disrupt the flight, and I don't give a fuck what anyone has to say about me if it does. He's not taking away the hours I plan to sit with her. No fucking way.

CHAPTER EIGHT
JADE

Holy shit, he's pissed. I can see him coming behind all the passengers down the center of the plane. How could I miss him? He's the big one with all the tattoos and bulging muscles that barely fit through the aisle. He's the one sending bullets through Harris before he even gets near.

At the risk of being in a fucking war zone, I tell Harris to switch me seats. He hasn't noticed Kaleb's face yet, so I know he's oblivious to what he's doing. I've been very careful about what Harris knows and thinks when it comes to Kaleb Maverick. He doesn't need to know Maverick single-handedly gave me the best fucks I've ever had. That even with the slight introduction to Harris' dick, I can tell there's no comparison. I also know I'd never let Harris treat me like Kaleb has. His domineering attitude is obnoxious, yet downright fucking sweltering to my core at the same time. I'd beat Harris across his fucking head if he tried half the shit Kaleb has done to me.

"I'd feel better having you in the middle, Elliott. You'll have more room to move your sore arm around if you do." Kaleb glares at both Harris and I. Shit, if looks could kill, we'd both be dead. Move my arm around, my goddamn ass. This is his way of staking his claim.

I'm not about to argue on an airplane full of people, so I switch with Harris. Simple as that. Screw it. I'm going to fall asleep, so he can huff, piss, and moan his arrogant ass to himself.

This flight will be interesting with these two sandwiching me in, that's for damn sure. Harris is bound to tease me like he always does, and Kaleb is going to get pissed about the banter between Harris and I. It's destined to be a horrible flight. The lack of oxygen is already overridden from fumes of testosterone. Someone knock me out now, please.

Harris and I struggle to switch seats, and I feel Kaleb staring at us. He's been in the aisle waiting for the switch, allowing us room to prevent bumping my sore arm. I appreciate his impatient patience, but he's going to have to chill.

We're finally settled just before Kaleb sits in the seat on my right. Both guys are wide in the shoulders, so I'm glad I halfway like them both, because they're taking up more than their own space.

We're all quiet as the rest of the passengers finish boarding, but I can feel the tension on my right. There's no doubt Kaleb could fuck something up right now, or in my case, fuck something hard.

He slides his ass forward in the seat, sitting lower in his chair and taking up even more leg room, with his leg against mine like he's marking his territory by touching me. I refuse to let him weigh heavy on me with a flight home in front of me. I should be ecstatic. I should be planning my stay and preparing to notify everyone of my return, but I'm not. My family doesn't even know where I've been. Hell, I'm not even sure I should call them before I walk in their door.

I need to though. Something is ticking away in the back of my head to contact my parents. I realize it has everything to do with me shooting a young child. No matter how I see it, he was someone's son, but he was a young man who was going to shoot Kaleb. Yet, I can't seem to get his young face out of my mind. I'd give anything to be able to have my dad hold me like he did when I was growing up. He'd comfort me when I fell off my bike or when my brother Jason thought it would be fun to sneak up behind me, tackle me to the ground, and put a pair of his underwear over my head. I hated that more than anything. No matter how many times he was told to knock it off, he tortured me every chance he got by pulling sick jokes.

I laugh out loud, recalling the day I got him back. He was sleeping. I crept into his room, scattered unused tampons all over his bed, and of course had to dip them in red paint for effect. He freaked the hell out when he woke up. All I could do was laugh my ass off when he wandered into my room the next morning. His face was beat red and he was so pissed. Then he cocked his head to the side when he saw me sitting at my vanity, applying the little bit of makeup I wore.

"After all these years you paid me back. It's about time you grew a set of balls." We laughed and joked around about the balls thing.

"I think I'll stick with what I have, thank you very much. Now, get the hell out of my room and keep your underwear off of my head, asshole, or next time I do pay you back, you'll really be sorry." At thirteen years old I had finally grown up, he had said as he walked out the door, laughing all the way to his room. Needless to say, after that night, I never saw a pair of his underwear again.

Shit, I miss him. I just wish I were going home to see him.

"What's so funny?" Harris leans into my space. His hand goes to my leg, squeezing it gently. I lean my head back, shifting my body to face him the best I can. Being careful not to put too much pressure on my sore arm. I feel the effects of the pain pills kicking in slightly, although I'm not quite ready to zone out yet.

I'm afraid to sleep. I'm terrified of the dreams I'll have. I try to tune those thoughts out and move a little closer to Harris to tell him the story. The entire time we're talking, with my body facing away from Kaleb, I can feel his anger, jealousy, and frustration poking holes in the back of my head. He's a ticking time bomb ready to go off at any second.

The truth is, I can't bear to look at the man. He makes me want to feel things I'm not ready for. Mainly him. If we had started off normal, like a date, or getting to know each other before we fucked without me even knowing his damn name, then who knows, maybe things could be different between us, but it can't be. He's my damn Commander. This shit is off-limits and completely against everything we both know. Whatever happened needs to be left here, or should I say, back in Afghanistan.

I'm not sure how long Harris and I talk, keeping everything low-key. I talk more about my past while he brings up the things he wants to do when he returns. As my eyes drift closed, my head falls onto his shoulder, and I swear I hear him ask me to dinner when we return. I'm also pretty sure I hear a low rumbling growl of "fuck no" from behind me.

KALEB

No fucking way is he taking her anywhere. This shit ends the minute we step off this plane. She may not have taken Harris' joke about spanking her ass seriously, but by god, the first chance I get, I'm spanking her ass. In fact, the more I think about it, the more it turns me on. I'm going to punish her in a way that will have her begging me to fuck her when I'm done. Then she'll learn not to ignore my ass. Or to treat me like I don't even exist. Fuck that.

I'm not sure what kind of game she's playing, but this guy never played nice in the sandbox, and I'll be damned if I start now. What's mine is mine and Harris needs to know she's off-limits for him.

Out of the corner of my eye I watch her sleep on his shoulder, her long blond hair enveloping her face. I glare at the motherfucker, who seems to be content with his head laid back and his eyes closed. He's fucking sleeping next to her.

What I need right the hell now is a few shots of whiskey to kill the burn that it's him and not me. Shit. I sound like a pussy, a defeated one at that.

"No!" She jolts up, scaring the shit out of me and several other people around us who gasp at her loud voice.

"Hey." I place my hand over the top of hers. Her head whips around in my direction. Harris wakes with her abruptness too, but I couldn't care less about him; my focus is on her.

"Are you alright, Miss?" The cute little flight attendant who has been flirting with me every time she walks past stops to ask.

"Yes. Bad dream. Sorry." Jade sits up. Shit. I don't even have to ask what she was dreaming about. I can see the agony in her eyes. She's suffering over what happened more than I thought she would.

"Come here, please." Removing my hand from hers and bringing it up and around her shoulder, I am careful not to cause her physical pain.

She's carrying so much anguish inside of her, and it kills me to see her like this. She may hate me for what I'm going to recommend to my superior when I return, but Jade needs help. She needs to talk to someone about this. Someone neutral. One of the Army's doctors who specialize in treating soldiers who have a difficult time when returning home from war or a mission.

I'm still her Commander, well technically not, but who gives a shit. I care about her and part of my job will be to discuss how everyone on my team performed. Jade did everything she was supposed to do, but this, this can't be ignored. They won't allow her to return or to recommend her for another mission anywhere if she can't handle what happened out there. I know how hard she has worked for this.

This is her life. It will destroy her if she can't handle it. She'll be behind a desk, shuffling papers or worse yet, she could be discharged. That, I know damn well she'd not be able to handle. Fuck.

She starts to relocate her tiny frame from dickfuck to me. As she does, I lift the armrest up, giving her the comfort she needs to rest her head on my shoulder. This is where she needs to be, even though I desperately want to kiss her, to run my fingers through her hair, and calm her. I know I can't, not yet anyway.

I play the part of her leader, letting her breathing calm. She stills in my arms, and I know she's fallen back to sleep. I sigh heavily then shift my gaze to Harris who is watching us, or should I say me, with confusion smeared all over his face.

"What?" I mouth dryly.

Those damn eyes of his give him away. He wants to know what the fuck I'm doing. Better yet, he wants to know why.

"Is she alright?" JJ questions from his seat across the aisle and a row back. I tear my scrutiny away from Harris. My attention spins in the opposite direction.

"She will be." That's really all I can say.

"I hope you're right." His reply is full of concern. He can't say anything more, either. By the way he's casting his look at her, I know the kid cares about her. He looks up to her. What man wouldn't? She's strong, courageous, and a damn fighter.

"Is she sleeping?" I whisper to him. I need to make sure before I spill my guts to Harris. JJ nods his head then stuffs his earbuds back into his ears, going back to the movie he was watching on the small monitor attached to the back of the seat in front of him.

"What the fuck is going on between you two and don't fucking lie to me." Harris snaps. Which no doubt has me teetering on the edge of grabbing him by the throat and telling him to shut his fucking mouth.

But I don't and I won't. What I will do is tell him what he needs to fucking hear. What he needs to know before we land and before he thinks for one damn second he's going to get anywhere near her once we've been cleared to go about our daily lives.

I decide to toy with him a little and play stupid.

"What the fuck are you talking about?" I whisper low. I'm not about to wake her up. This is out of line on his part, and he damn well knows it. Not that I have room to talk about being out of line.

"Don't play dumb, Maverick. I'm not as fucking oblivious as you think. I see the way you look at her. You want her." His tone is arrogant.

"This isn't the time or the place to have this discussion." I let my stare challenge him to say more.

"I don't see why not. Look around. There isn't a single person paying attention to you having your arms around her except me." His brows lift.

I contemplate my answer. Do I tell him or not? If I do, I risk the chance of him opening his mouth to Jade, letting her know he knows. Or worse, telling someone of rank that could ruin my career and hers. If I don't, he'll go after her. He's a man like me, who goes after what he wants, and we both know he wants her for more than a quick fuck. She's the only one who is blind and can't see it.

She sees him as her friend. A friend whom, thank god, I stopped before they fucked. Before he used that fuck to get under her skin. The difference between Harris and I is, I went after what I wanted the first chance I got. Where he's had years to tell her how he's felt about her. Years he wasted. He fucked up.

This woman lying in my arms, sleeping on my shoulder, is right where she is meant to be. With me. I'm going to have to fight tooth and nail to make her see it. I may have fought hard on every mission I've been on, every deployment I went to and I know damn well she'll be worth the fight.

There is nothing I will fight harder for than her. I need her as much as she needs me. And I'll be damned if a man who isn't man enough to tell a woman how he feels about her will stand in my way.

"You want the truth, Harris? Here's the truth. She's mine." I growl the words through a whisper, hoping she doesn't wake up. He's somewhat shocked, but his expression is angrier than anything.

"It's funny how she doesn't seem to acknowledge that herself." He leans closer, making sure I hear him. "She's not something that I'll walk away from, and she's sure as fuck not someone I'll let get into something that's going to hurt her. Let me ask you, Commander, why exactly was Jade's back full of bloody scrapes and scratches?" I look toward the stewardess coming down the middle aisle, not wanting to get into it with him. Why can't he just understand that I'm not fucking around here?

"What Jade and I do is none of your fucking business."

"That's where you're dead fucking wrong. If she gets hurt, I feel obligated to find justice in who wronged her. If you're some fucked-up asshole who gets off on making people bleed, you just need to walk the fuck away from her. Consider it saving your own life."

"That's not how it is." I look down to her sleeping peacefully on my shoulder. Christ. I really don't give a shit what his opinion of me is. It's her I care about. Her opinion matters. She has to know I want more than sex with her. I've told her this.

"Look, I have nothing but respect for you as a leader and a soldier, but Jade is not an area I'll settle on. She deserves happiness. If you're what causes that, then you'll have my full support, but if I see one fucking tear in her eye that you caused.... Be prepared to meet me for your day of reckoning."

"I can work with that." Because the last thing I want to see is another tear escape her gorgeous eyes.

"And don't fucking claim her like a piece of property. She's a human being, a strong one at that, who can make her own decisions. And until she tells me she's taken, I'll be right beside her, just being me."

I want to like the man who went to battle with me to take down one of the most notorious terrorists of all time, but this guy is choosing to go to war with me now.

"Harris, don't kid yourself, you don't stand a chance in a war with me. I'll ruin you. I'll make you disappear into the depths of hell on a fucking mission you'd rather die than finish."

"And I'll climb out of that hell to come find you if you so much as put another fucking scratch on her porcelain body." We may disagree on who should hold her at night, but we agree on Jade's safety. I want her happy too, and I will do my best to make sure she recovers from the nightmares she's bound to have." I swallow hard and take in the words he's saying. If she comes with me, I'll do everything in my power to make sure she's not hurt.

"I can respect that," I say truthfully.

"Good. I'm glad we could see eye to eye." He sits back finally, looking straight ahead at his monitor, and stuffs those earbuds in his ears. Keep them there, asshole; and you will stay the hell away from her.

CHAPTER NINE
JADE

The jolt of the plane landing wakes me up. I'm incredibly warm and definitely not sleeping on a soft pillow. No, what I'm lying on is hard, but damn, I'm right where a part of me wants to be though. His smell gives him away. He's all man. Rough, rugged, and tough man that's easy to feel safe near. When I open my eyes, I see one of my legs is curled up underneath me, my inured arm is sprawled across his chest, and my head is lying on his shoulder. God, he feels good with his arm wrapped around me, caging me in tight to his body. I go to move, my body aching to stretch. I'm pulled tighter into him. My mind wonders how I went from falling asleep on Harris's shoulder to Kaleb's.

"Hey, sleepyhead." His voice is raspy. He must've fallen asleep too.

"Hey." I jerk out of his hold, realizing what I've done. My eyes dart to Harris, who is sleeping. I hope he missed just how sprawled across Kaleb I was. I roll my neck around and stretch my legs out the best I can, trying to regain feeling in my limbs from this long flight.

"Those must be some killer pain pills. You were out and you snore." They must be. I still wonder how I went from Harris to him. Kaleb chuckles as he stretches his arms over his head, those tattoos pulling taut when his muscles flex in his upper arms. Right now, I don't care how I shifted my body in my sleep. He's a distraction. One I'm not sure if I want to eat off of, or choke on.

Shit. I would love to finally get a close-up of every one of those tattoos. I wonder if he'll ever tell me the meaning behind them. And don't even let me forget about those damn abs. His thin t-shirt doesn't leave a damn thing to the imagination, not that my mind will let me forget them. They're hard, defined, and bulging through his t-shirt, and I can still feel the ripple on my fingertips from when I was sprawled across him like a desperate magnet.

In spite of sleeping for the most part of the flight, I'm still exhausted. All I want to do is go home, take a long, hot shower and sleep for days. Then wake up and figure out what in the hell I'm going to do with my time off. I need a distraction, anything to help me keep my troubled mind off of that boy.

"He's right, you do snore. Loud." My head swings around to Harris.

"What the fuck ever. Like the two of you don't." I roll my eyes at him.

"I will the minute I hit my bed, that's for damn sure." JJ leans forward, stretching. He looks worse than I feel, which says a lot, because I feel like shit.

"Won't we all." Harris looks at me, then to Kaleb. The way he glares at Kaleb has a red flag instantly waving in my face. Something happened while I was sleeping, I can feel it. The tension between these two has hardened. Damn them. I'm not in the mood for whatever kind of bullshit these two have going on between them, and if Kaleb said anything about what happened between the two of us, he'll wish to god I didn't save his ass, because I will kill him myself. Even though it will be a long time before I even think about having sex with another man, there could never be anything between the two of us. We're entirely different.

I'm not a prude, that's blatantly obvious by the way I let him fuck me in every hole he could, but we aren't even on the same page when it comes to sex. The cheeks of my ass clench together when I think of the way he roughly took what he wanted, his demanding ways making me submit to him. God, I'd be lying if I didn't love every minute of it. The way he touched me, fucked me like he could never get enough.

I need to get the hell away from him and have some me time. I could hit the clubs with my girlfriend Mallory. Anything to make me forget him. It's been way too long since I've done something for myself, but when the Army is your life and you've done nothing but train for the past few years to set goals to fulfill your dreams, going out is the last thing on your mind. I haven't had time to myself in I don't know how long.

"Let's get out of here." Kaleb extends his hand out to me as soon as the airplane comes to a stop. He helps me stand, and I stretch more, holding my sore arm tight against me. The pain has faltered some, leaving me with a slight discomfort, but it's nothing I can't handle. The pain pills will help. I drop his hand the minute I step out into the aisle, making him frown.

"Just go," my cranky ass tells him. I watch him and chastise my stupid hormones the entire way off the plane, all the way down the hallway. Stupid woman. Why did you taste the forbidden? He's ruined you for a long time.

"You're riding with me." He grabs my hand again like we're a damn couple as we walk through the airport after saying goodbye to JJ and Harris.

Harris seemed distant, his hug brief, no smart-ass comment like he usually drops either.

"What happened between you and Harris, Kaleb?" I jerk my hand from his when we exit the door. The sweet smell of Florida hits my senses immediately. The tang of the salty air has me breathing it in. I'm home. American soil has never felt so good.

"I'll tell you when we get to my Jeep." I can't help but laugh, don't ask me why. I never gave a thought as to what kind of vehicle he might drive. Hell, I never thought about anything except the way he fucked me and the way he made me feel. A part of me wants to know everything I can about him, while the rational part of me knows I shouldn't.

"God, your laugh is beautiful." He stares down at me. For the first time since I met him, I feel my skin blush. It's strange being able to hear those words from him, knowing he can speak his mind now without having to hide anything. I'm at a loss for words.

"Thank you," I reply politely and feel extremely uncomfortable. This is so unlike me. I know I need a ride to the base to get my evaluation done and tell my superior officer what happened to me. I'll need to fill him in on how well Kaleb guided us through our mission, like the great leader he is.

It's a half-hour drive, and I'm worried about spending that much time with Kaleb. I'm afraid of the things he'll say. He made it perfectly clear in the hospital that he wants to explore what he thinks we have once we return home, and now that we have, I wish I would have told him I wasn't riding with him. I know damn well both Harris and JJ would have taken me.

I follow him across the street into the parking garage, keeping my eyes off of his tempting ass and the strong muscles across his back. He's mouthwatering. He's dangerous, and if I don't stay the hell away from him, he could destroy me. All he wants from me is a fuck. With the kind of man he is, I could easily fall for him. I may be strong, a soldier trained to harden both her inner and outer shell, but there isn't any amount of training that can guard my heart. He would break me. Shatter me. I can't have that. Especially with everything going on right now.

"Nice," I say when we stroll up to a white older model Jeep. "This is my girl. 1979 CJ5. My parents bought it for me when I was sixteen. I love this thing." He pulls out a set of keys from his pocket and unlocks my door before tossing our bags in the back.

"I like it, it's you." He turns toward me, crossing his arms over his massive chest. His gaze turns instantly dark. "Is that a compliment, Jade?" I study him. My mind is so foggy and the effects of the pain pill have to be lingering still; there is no way the woman that I am wouldn't have a smartass comeback waiting to snap back.

"Kaleb. I merely said it's you. Which means it's manly. Nothing more." His lips twitch. Why is this so strange?

"You're a shit liar, Jade. There's more. There will always be more. This wall you've suddenly built around yourself will not stop me. You know damn well I have the sources to blow that wall to shreds, to make it shatter. I have no clue what's running through that gorgeous head of yours, but we will be talking. You will listen and most importantly, Jade, you will become mine." He's speaking to me as if he's still my Commander, and I don't like it at all. Finally, I feel Jade swim to the surface, plunging her way through the murky waters and ready to show her true self.

"You don't own me. No one does. No one ever will. And if I decide I want to be in a relationship, it sure as hell won't be with a man like you." I'm so angry right now. I go to move past him, but he reaches out to draw me close to him. He wraps his arms around my waist carefully. I sigh out of frustration. This arrogant bastard will not listen to a word I say, and it's pissing me the fuck off. All he had to say was I will become his and the fog lifted from within my head. Like I'm something that can be owned.

"I don't want to own you. I want you to be yourself. To see you smile, laugh like you did back there when I told you I drove a Jeep. I want to surprise you with shit like that. To turn your world upside down, to drive you insanely mad with desire. Then turn around and fill that desire with everything I've got to please you. I know you can't get this shit through your thick skull, but goddamn it, Jade. How many times do I have to tell you that it's more than sex? I want us to get to know each other. Jesus Christ, what the hell are you hiding from?" I stand stoic. His words shock me to the middle of my chest. How can I tell him I have no idea what I'm afraid of when I don't even know myself? Maybe it's the way whatever this is between us started off. I knew the man for five minutes before I had his dick slamming into my pussy, making me want to yell out like a crazy woman.

Then it hits me, my brainwaves working overtime. I'm a slut. I let a man fuck me every way he could without knowing a damn thing about him. Without giving a second thought to the way I would feel about myself when we returned home. He knows everything about me, and I don't know a damn thing about him, except for the little bit he told me. How can he stand here and not see me this way? Not see me as the slut I am? I feel tears pricking my eyes and I hate it. I hate the woman who has returned home. When I left here trained and prepared, I never thought I would come back broken and weak. This isn't me at all.

I pull away from him somehow and try to find some sort of strength to speak.

"Kaleb, I'm not hiding from anything. I'm scared. With everything that's happened between us and then I shot that child. I can't think straight." My hands fly up to my head, squeezing the sides as the pounding headache travels from the back of my head around to the front.

"Come on then. I won't push you anymore about us for right now, but I won't give up, so you'll have to deal with it eventually. I want you. What I will push you on, Jade, is that you talk to someone about what happened out there. I can't help you with that. You may be pissed off, but I'm recommending that you do. Now let's go get this over with so I can take you home." He pushes himself off from the Jeep and extends his hand out to me to guide me up and in. All I can think about as I watch him walk around the front, climb in, stick the keys in the ignition, and crank his so-called baby on, is going home.

Our drive is relatively quiet. The raspy voice of Jimi Hendrix lulls me to relax in the seat. Although my brain won't shut up, the dread of telling my superior what he already knows has my head throbbing worse than it did. Kaleb is right. I need to talk to someone. A neutral person. I may be screwed up over what I've done. However, I'm not oblivious to the fact I could use some help. I know good and well it will be recommended to me. I sigh heavily. I want nothing more than to be myself. God, after this mission and the things I've done, I don't even know who I am anymore.

By the time we pull up to the gate and show our identity badges to the officer, I'm a mess.

"Can I drive you home?" Kaleb asks after he parks.

"I'm too tired to make the drive to Jacksonville tonight. I thought I would get a hotel." It's the truth. I'm starving, and as much as I would love to sleep in my own bed, the thought of driving tonight doesn't appeal to me; besides, he needs his rest as much as I do.

"Jade. I have a place fifteen minutes from here. Like hell you're staying at a hotel. Wait for me here if you're done before me." His eyes smolder over with intensity, and I feel a twinge inside. Jesus. I'm doomed. There goes my rebellious body again, thinking for me and defying every rule I've made for him.

"Okay." My response feels so awkward. This entire situation feels that way. The freedom to say what we want, to even have a civil conversation, is strange. I really don't want to stay at his place. It feels too personal. To extreme. Hell, maybe I should request treatment in the hospital, or say goodbye now. I should just walk away, but I can't. Instead, I follow him inside, where he goes one way and I go another.

"I'm going to request you see one of our doctors, Jade." I knew this was coming. I'm okay with it. I know I need it. Maybe it will help me cope with what I've done.

"I agree, Sir. I'll make an appointment right away." Reaching across his dark wooden table, I retrieve the card from his outstretched hand.

"You did well out there. Now go. Make sure you call the first chance you get. I'm not clearing you for active duty until I receive a report back from the psychiatrist." He stands and straightens out his uniform before walking with purpose to the side of his desk.

"I sure will." I rise and salute him. He shakes his head, leaving me somewhat dumbfounded.

"It's me who should salute you. I'm proud of you, Captain." His shiny shoes click together. I suppress my joy from being saluted by a General in the United States Army. I spin on my feet and exit the door with the first honest to god genuine smile on my face since I left this country.

"You ready?" Kaleb is standing against the brick wall, tapping away on his phone when I walk out into the warm early evening air.

"Yes. Starving too." Feeling somewhat energized after my briefing, I decide to make the best of my time with Kaleb.

"Good. I ordered a pizza. You okay?" My breath catches in my throat when he shoves off of the wall and places one of his strong, sturdy arms around my shoulder before he starts to steer us toward his Jeep. He's powerful in the way he walks and in the way he moves. I've already admitted I was scared, of what, I'm not sure. Him. Me. Or hell, it could be both.

"Holy shit. This is you? It's beautiful, Kaleb." I point to the cream-colored stucco home in front of me. It sits in a fancy private estate called Lowell Estates.

"Yup. Home, baby." Oh hell, his dangerous smile glistens as his eyes rake up and down my body when he opens the door, those devious baby blues never leaving my face. Not even when he reaches behind us and pulls out our bags. Not even when he walks in front of and around his Jeep. Or when he opens the door to help me out. The only time he takes them off of me is when he slides his key into the lock, swings the door open, and drops the bags on the floor to take the pizza from my trembling hand.

I have no time to think. No time to breathe before he gently guides me back with one hand placed in the center of my chest. My heart is thumping away with so much desire, or it could be nerves, or hell maybe even anticipation? I feel him kick the door closed with his booted foot before he gracefully lifts me in his arms. "Kaleb, what are you doing?" He needs to put me down. His strides are determined. "I'm taking you where I've wanted you since the first time I saw you. To my bed."

"We can't do this, Kaleb. There are things we need to talk about." I'm on emotional overload here. This needs to end. If he gets me in his bed, I may never want to leave, and I have to. I need my head cleared, get my shit together. And I need to do it without him.

"We can and we are. We can talk later, Jade." He pushes onward, walking over the threshold of what I assume is his bedroom. It's dark, but oh hell, does his scent hit me the minute he lays me down on his bed. His smell is everywhere. I inhale deeply, the aroma shooting straight to my core and god help me, I know I'm going to regret this when we're done. I'd be fooling myself if I didn't admit that I do want him in a bed where I can worship him, taste him, lick those abs, and trace my fingers around those tattoos on his chest. My body starts burning up, and the ache between my legs intensifies.

"Kaleb," I whisper. I can't see him; the sharp gruff awareness of his heavy breathing is all I can hear.

"I'm right here. Give us this. I know you're nervous; hell, so am I. This is real life. No more fighting. It's awkward, it all feels different, but I promise you, Jade, I'm not going to give up. Not when I know that you want this is as bad as I do." He sounds hungry. Almost as if this is a craving for him and he's finally getting the chance to fulfill it.

Then I feel his rough hands slide across my feet, removing my shoes. The end of the bed dips, and his hands slide up my jean-covered legs. I swallow when the warmth of his fingers practically burns a damn hole in my jeans.

"I want you," I say, and I do, even if it's the last time.

CHAPTER TEN
KALEB

Motherfucker. She's pulling away from me. The entire ride I felt the vibes coming off of her, distancing herself further away. She's living in her head. The last thing I should be doing right now is taking her to bed, but goddamn it, I can't help myself. I need her.

I may be crazy for rushing this, but Christ, this is what we do best. The second our bodies connect, it's like dynamite exploding. I need to remember to make her understand that this is only the beginning of us.

I'm not a man to force myself on a woman, that's why I need to hear her say she wants me. The talking shit can come later. Right now, I want to show her exactly what she does to me. I want to make her see that I'm not only out to fuck her. This time, I'm taking my time. I want to feel every inch of her skin. I want her to tell me how she feels when I have my cock buried deep into her. When I have her begging me for more.

I slide my hands up her legs, pushing her thighs apart when I reach them. Her little whimpers have my cock damn near bursting through the zipper of my pants. Fuck. She's in my bed. The urge to turn on the light so I can see her has me stopping at the sweet junction between her thighs, but I fight it. I'm too damn scared to take my hands off of her for fear she'll change her mind.

"Fucking hell, Jade. The heat between your legs has me craving you. I need to taste you." I unsnap her jeans, and she lifts her ass up to help me guide them down her legs, my fingers itching to feel her bare skin against mine the whole time.

"Oh god," she moans out the instant I grab her panties and tug them off right along with her jeans, tossing them over my shoulder. I trail my hands back up her legs. She's silky smooth, and by the time I reach her bare pussy, she's panting and drenched.

"Kaleb." That sexy as fuck voice of hers is dripping with want.

"Feel, Jade. Tell me you want me." I know I sound desperate. Maybe I am. I don't care. I have her alone in my house, finally. The smell of her arousal hits my nose and has my mouth watering. Fuck, I want to taste her on my lips, and I can't wait to have her come all over my beard.

"I do. I want you." Her words are barely a whisper. I've never heard anything in my life that's meant more to me than hearing what I've wanted to hear come out of her sexy little mouth.

I spread her legs wide. Those erotic noises she's making drive me out of my fucking mind. She can scream all she wants here. I welcome it, hell, I've been looking forward to it.

The first swipe of my tongue across her addicting clit has me losing control. I grip her ass with both of my hands, lift her up, and bury my face deep into her. I lick around her nub, sucking it deep into my mouth. "Oh fuck!" she screams. That's all it takes to ignite me. My tongue works her, licking, tasting, and devouring her. My beard becomes coated with her. My tongue soaks up every sweet piece of her. I own this pussy. It's mine.

When she squirms and the muscles in her ass clench, I know she's close. I set her back down on the bed, careful not to hurt her arm. My thumb presses on her clit, and when she explodes in my mouth as she screams my name, I swear to Christ I almost come in my goddamn pants.

"I'm not sure I'm prepared for what you do to me." I inhale her scent one more time before lifting my face.

"I know exactly what you mean, Kaleb." Her pussy is just as addicting as her smartass mouth and her eyes. Every part of her is an addiction that spreads through my veins, landing in the center of my chest.

Shoving myself off the bed, I make quick work of taking off my jeans and t-shirt. Thank god I'm a man who hates having his cock confined in a pair of briefs. I hated wearing them in the desert, but thank fuck I did, because every damn time I saw her out there, my cock got hard. But here at home, fuck no. I have no problem walking around hard as steel, letting her see exactly what she does to me.

"Come here," I demand.

"You come here," she challenges.

"I want your damn shirt off, smartass. Sit up."

"Oh." She chuckles. Then she does what she's told.

"I'm desperate to feel your skin against mine, Jade." Lifting her shirt up over her head, I'm careful not to hurt her.

"I want to feel you too." Yeah I thought it was impossible for my cock to get any harder. I think the bastard grew another inch from hearing her say that.

I reach around and find the clasp of her bra. I know it's sexy as fuck by the way the lace feels on my fingers. I slide it over her bandage, down her arms, flinging it over my shoulder, and my hands go to straight to her breasts. I pinch her nipples, tugging at them before drawing them into my mouth. She arches her back as her breathing spirals out of control. She can deny this shit all she wants, there is no damn way this connection we have is just about sex. The sex is a bonus. It's her heart I want and can feel in the pulse on her neck when I spread my hand gently around her throat. I want her heart.

"God, yes, Kaleb." I can't resist her. I need inside her now. Especially when she says my name. I'll never be tired of hearing her say it.

"Lie back." My words are hard. I need to be under control here when I glide my cock into her pussy. She may be filled with want right now, but god, she's fragile, not just her arm, but her mind. Her indifference with where we're headed collides with my determination to make her mine. She needs slow, yet hard. And fuck me if my cock isn't harder than it's ever been in my goddamn life. The thought of her underneath me has my balls squeezing my spine.

"Spread your legs." She does greedily.

"Kaleb. I need you right now." My eyes close. I need to soak in the fact that she is speaking freely. She can say my name whenever she wants. This shit is fucking real. She's in *my* bed.

"Say my name again." Gripping hold of my cock, leaning down on top of her, I wait for her response.

"Kaleb," she whispers. I line up to her, slowly sliding inside. I need to feel her. This isn't a quick fuck for us. Not this time.

"God, Kaleb, you feel so good."

"I don't want to hear anything but my name coming out of your mouth until we're done. You get me?" I capture her mouth with mine and move my cock in and out of her, her hips meeting every thrust. I dig my hands into the mass of blond hair I can't wait to see spread across my pillow.

"Kaleb." She unravels me as I pound into her hard and fast, then slow and gentle, my movements meant to drive her wild. Then her nails claw down my back, and her hands grab my ass and pull me into her as far as I can go.

I fucking lose it. Her hips thrust up to meet mine. Her pussy is so warm and tight, pulsing with every thrust of my cock. All I want to do is cherish her, and embrace her in my arms, and do right by her.

I can tell Jade has other plans; she wants to fuck. Her cries pleading for me to drive in harder and faster override my plans to go slow. When she bites into my shoulder, I hiss, and my cock swells even more. It blows up like a goddamn balloon, and I yell out her name as I still my cock deep in her and come so goddamn hard I swear to Christ if she weren't hurt, I could fuck her again.

I'm not pulling out, not this time. I keep my arms braced around her head and experience the deep-seated feeling of my cock still inside of her. Our breathing is rapid and our pulses flicker like a trapped animal's.

Even through the darkness I can feel her eyes on mine. Her thoughts are soaring. She's scared, I get it. The words are on the tip of my tongue to tell her we have time to figure this out, that

I'm as scared as she is, but I keep quiet until she nudges me without speaking. I shuffle off of her, catching my own thoughts, tucking them away until we can actually talk.

I roll onto my side and slide her into my arms. I hold her like this for a few minutes before she starts to pull away.

"I need to use your bathroom." She slides off the bed and instantly, her warmth is missing against my body. I decide to get up too, only grabbing the pizza before I return. She slides back into bed right after me.

"This room is definitely not you, Kaleb. Who decorated it?" We've finished off the pizza with a few beers, lying naked in my bed. Jade and her mouth demanded we get up so she could see my house. It's late, I'm so damn tired that I can barely keep my eyes open while Jade all of a sudden has a second wind. Mix the time difference and the fact she slept pretty much the entire flight, it's no wonder she's wound up.

Even though I'm tired as fuck, it doesn't slip past me that this is the second time she's mentioned something is or isn't me. She's fooling herself, not me.

"My mom and sister," I answer through a yawn.

"Well, I love it." I shrug. I've never paid any attention to the way they decorated my home before. All I did was tell them no girly shit. No pink or purple and they could do whatever the hell they wanted. They had a damn field day, and I paid a hefty price for this dark cherry wood king size bed with matching nightstands and two dressers. It was their idea for the brown walls. I look around then notice the cream-colored vase with white orchids on a stand in the corner. My lips quirk into a smile.

"Why do you say it doesn't look like me?" I tease then run my fingers up her bare thigh. Why the hell she has that sheet covering her perfect tits, I have no idea. My hand is halfway curled, ready to yank it off of her when she shocks the fuck out of me.

"I need time away, Kaleb. I'm going to make a call to the doctor, visit her if I can tomorrow, and then I'm going to go see my parents." What the hell? I thought she wasn't in a hurry to see her parents.

"I'll take you."

"No, Kaleb. I need to get away. I need time to think, and I can't do it when I know damn well you won't let me."

"We live three hours away from each other, Jade. I have a job. How the hell is that not letting you have the space you need when we won't see each other every day?" Fuck, I'm so damn frustrated and tired. This is not what I want to discuss. I'll give her the space she needs, even though it's not what I think she needs, or they aren't whom she needs. She needs me. I should be the one helping her. They may be her family, but I know through all the research I did on her that they haven't been close since the day she enlisted.

"Go see them then. Just don't shut me out." I lean into her, her eyes bleeding with unspoken words.

"Let's get some sleep." She reaches up and tugs on my beard, detouring the answer I need to hear.

A nagging feeling sits in the pit of my gut after I shut off the light and draw her into my arms. Why the hell do I have the feeling she's trying to tell me goodbye?

I know she's gone before I even open my eyes. We fell asleep with me holding her close, and now as I tilt my head to the side she was sleeping on, she's gone. Obviously, she called someone to pick her up. I'll be damned if I chase after her. I've laid it all out the best I can. The rest is up to her. I may care about her, but I sure as hell won't push her into something she claims she isn't ready for.

Stretching my sore body before I climb out of bed, I feel the burn of pulling my muscles taut surging through my veins. God, it feels good to be home. Even though I was only gone for a week or so, it seems like forever. Christ, I stink like foreign soil. I showered in Germany, but there isn't anything like a shower in your own home.

Tossing the covers off, I clamber my still tired ass into my bathroom, crank the knob in my walk- in shower, and take a piss while the water warms. The quiet is such a reprieve from the sound of gunshots, bombs, and screaming men and women from a few days ago. You would think I would be used to this kind of shit. Truth is, you never get used to seeing someone's brains being splattered all over the place. Or a woman screaming at you for killing the man she loves.

War takes its toll on every damn part of the body. The sleepless nights tossing and turning on a cot that's not only uncomfortable as hell but way too damn small for the body. The brain is working overtime, everyone scared out of their goddamn minds. It never gets easier. The reward behind doing the job you were delegated and trained to do is what gives you the will to survive, knowing you're keeping your country and the citizens safe from the perils of the enemy.

That's my biggest reason right there for not calling Jade. She needs to deal with what happened, in her own way. On her own time. I'll give her a week or so before I find her. The first time is the hardest of them all. It doesn't matter how much they psychoanalyze your brain; drill a damn hole in your head and fill it with the fact that the enemy will kill you unless you strike first. It's a vicious circle that spins inside of you until you blow it up your own damn self.

I lean my head forward in the shower, letting the steam and the hot water clear my mind. I learned a long time ago to let that shit go. It's my job. I do it well, and I'll do it again if the need arises.

I grab my soap and scrub the hell out of my body, washing away the last traces of this mission. No more. I'm done thinking about it until I help her.

After drying off and finishing my morning routine, I throw on a pair of worn jeans and a navy t-shirt. Slipping into my boots, I make my way down the hall and to the kitchen, leaving my bed unmade. It may be unusual that I don't want to make it. I don't give a shit. The idea of knowing she was in my bed at all makes me want to leave it all crumpled to hell.

"Hey, fuckhead!" I shout into the phone where I placed it on the counter before walking to the other side of the kitchen to grab a bottle of water out of the fridge. It's eleven in the morning, too damn late for coffee.

"Fuck off. Wait, you've been fucking off for a week now. Get your ass in here so I can leave and find me some hot piece of ass to take home and fuck." Some things will never change. I shake my head as I listen to my partner carrying on about how deprived his dick has been since I've been gone. He's so full of fucking shit. That man will fuck any goddamn thing. He's a hundred times worse than I've ever been. My desire to pick up other women vanished the minute I saw Jade. I shake her from my mind and chug down the entire bottle of water, toss the empty plastic into the garbage, snatch the phone off of the counter, and head out the front door. "Whatever, fucker. I'll be there in a few," I tell him before I end the call in the middle of him bitching.

I stare down at my phone. The urge to call her is grinding away at my gut. Instead, I toss the phone into the empty passenger seat and grab my shades and my ball cap. I'm giving her the space she asked for, for now anyway.

CHAPTER ELEVEN
JADE

I knew the moment I woke up drenched in sweat, my entire body trembling from the nightmare that won't leave my damn mind, that I had to leave. It didn't matter that the sun was set to rise. I had to get the hell out of there before I woke him. The man has been through enough shit to have to deal with a wacked-out woman who can't handle what she has been trained to do. I don't need coddled, or for anyone to tell me I will be alright. I need to do this my way.

So what did I do? Like a coward, I fumbled through the dark of his bedroom. Found all of my clothes and tiptoed out of his room. Found a half bath in the hallway and quickly got dressed, picked up my bag from the floor where he dropped it, and quietly exited his house. Called a cab to pick me up. My eyes stayed glued to his front door, praying he wouldn't notice I was gone. It wasn't until I pulled away that I let out a deep breath he didn't wake. Not that I wouldn't have left anyway, but I couldn't deal with seeing the look on his face. He wants to help, I appreciate him for that. But how can anyone help me if I don't try to help myself?

By the time the cab driver dropped me off to retrieve my car, my nerves were frantic and my chest was so very tight. Every noise had me jumping. It was like gunfire to my ears, strangling me and making it hard to breathe, not to mention hard to drive. Turning on the radio to some random classical station to drown out the noises from outside, I made my way down the road and away from Commander Kaleb Maverick.

By the time I made the three-hour drive to my apartment, thankful my roommate was already gone to work, I was a mess and coated in sweat. My chest was aching to the point I felt like I was having a heart attack as anxiety swarmed around me.

By the time I was inside my apartment, my hands were shaking so bad I dropped the card my superior officer handed me on the floor twice before falling to my knees in a crying mess.

Through tear-stained eyes I managed to dial the psychiatrist's number. I attempted to gain some sort of control before speaking to her receptionist, but not enough that she didn't recognize the panic in my voice before she placed me on hold, returning shortly to tell me to be there within the hour.

So here I am. Sitting in the office of Doctor Simone Randall. Her office is cheery and bright. Her coal-black hair is pulled back with those old metal clips on each side like my grandmother used to use. Her eyes are kind and sympathetic. She's not showing me pity, just warmth and understanding, as if she knows exactly what I've been through. This is the first time I feel a sliver of hope.

"We both know what's brought you here today, Jade. Anything you tell me stays between the two of us. It's strictly confidential. My report back to your superior officer will only state whether I feel you need more time or whether you're ready to perform your job duties," she says honestly.

"Thank you," I tell her.

"I haven't had the chance to look over much of this. To be quite honest, I wasn't expecting to hear from you for a few days. However, my job is to help you and listen to you. You tell me where you want to start. I'll stop you if I have questions." I'm in love with her already. Don't ask me how I know this. Maybe it's her non-judgmental demeanor or the clarity in her tone. I don't know, but when I start to tell her how difficult it is for me to handle the fact that I shot a young boy, her words back to me make sense. It's something I knew all along, but hearing it from a person who wasn't out there, or from someone who thinks they know what's best for me, puts a whole new perspective on my troubling mind.

"I think it's good for you that you have some time off and stay away from the base where it's going to remind you of the trauma you've endured. However, I would like to recommend you not isolate yourself from everyone. Nightmares are going to come and go, Jade, and with those nightmares comes the difficulty of sleeping." Then she surprises me with her next request. My brain desperately tries to understand why she thinks this would help me.

"One thing I did see in your file is that you lost a brother. Would you like to talk about that at all?" I'm not sure if I do. That's one of the reasons why I need to make peace with my parents. Why I need to feel normal before I make the drive across town to see them. My older brother Jason committed suicide almost two years ago after his second tour in Iraq. He hid his symptoms of PTSD from us all. The police found him two days later, after he took his life by jumping off a bridge. It destroyed my parents; a part of all of us died that day with Jason.

By the time I've left her office with another appointment for the day after tomorrow and a mild anti-anxiety prescription, I know exactly the first place I need to go to begin this journey of healing.

"I'm here, Jason." I am kneeling on the ground in front of my brother's grave. There's just enough light left on the horizon for me to see his name engraved and the words 'Forever in our Hearts' below his name.

"I'm sorry it's been so long. I don't have an excuse, and I won't make one up. I miss you." I trace my fingers over his name. The tears fall freely and I let them.

"I'm struggling, Jason. I need you to give me strength to get through this. You already know what happened, what I did. There's no need for me to tell you. I love my job and what it stands for. I would kill that young boy all over again to save my team. It's just... I can't get the image of how young he was out of my head. It's haunting my soul. It's tragic and I'm scared." My forehead goes to the cold stone and I cry. I'm so tired, weak, and drained.

I'm not sure how long I stay there with my head up against his headstone with fond memories imploring my mind. It's dark on a warm night with a million stars in the sky by the time I gather myself and thank my brother for listening. It's a figment of my imagination upon walking away when I hear his speech reaffirm what I already know.

"You'll get there, Jade. The hardest part about war is the battle we have within ourselves. We struggle with it daily. For some it may never go away, but for you it will. You have to believe it, believe in yourself, believe in your country, and don't shut people out."

I turn my phone on the minute I get into my car, checking my messages before I leave to go see my parents. I'm surprised when there is one from Harris, and one from my roommate, and none from Kaleb. A part of me is hurt that he never called or texted to check up on me, while the other part is somewhat relieved. Maybe he's going to give me the space I asked for and let me figure this out on my own.

I check the voicemail from Mallory first. *"I'm going to kick your ass. How dare you come home and not call me first? You better call me right now, Jade Elliott, or I will snap your tiny ass in two. Call me now!"* I laugh at her obnoxious behavior. The bitch knows how this shit works. Hell, her father is a retired officer from the Navy. I listen to Harris' message through my Bluetooth as I pull out of the cemetery, eager to see my parents.

"Hey. I'm heading to my ranch in Alabama for the weekend. Thought maybe a change of scenery might do you good. Call me if you'd like to go." That's it. Short and to the point. No flirtation in his tone at all. I know Harris all too well. My intuition about him knowing there is something going on between Kaleb and I is spot on. Kaleb told him. I know he did, and I should wring his thick, muscular, corded neck for opening his big mouth, but instead I feel relieved. I'm not in the mood for Harris and his sexual advances. What I am in the mood for is a nice weekend away. Riding horses, which I've never done before in my life.

Dialing Mallory, I prepare for the chaos of her excitement. She's exactly whom I need to be around right now, but she's the one person, who can read straight through my emotions. She'll never ask specifics; she'll just get that I've had a rough time.

"Did you really wait twenty-four hours to check in with me? Jade Elliott, there'd better be a story about one hot night of sex as an explanation of yourself."

"Hi Mal, I'm home." I avoid her interrogation and try to move the conversation along. I'm going to keep everything I've been through with Maverick to myself. She'd get caught up in the would-haves and should-haves and drive me insane.

"Tell me you're on your way here now! I'm going to take the next few days off if you are." Mal may get excited about things and cause me to internally flinch at her energy, but honestly, she's exactly what I need right now. Girl time will do me wonders after being around so much constant testosterone.

"I'm going to stop by my parents' house for a few days maybe. But what I really need to do is stand my ass in a hot shower for hours."

"Your parents?" She knows this is a very awkward situation for me and that I haven't spoken with them in a while. It's been nearly two years since Jason's funeral, and I think I've only talked to them twice. I just couldn't handle looking at the loss in my mom's eyes when my heart matched her emotions exactly. I know she was worried I'd turn up the same, but what she doesn't understand is, I was already just like Jason before he died. There's not possibly any way I could become more like the guy I looked up to my entire childhood. He was my hero. He fought for my country and for my freedom.

He would share stories with me he wouldn't share with anyone else. I was his outlet and through all of that, we shared a closeness I've never felt with either of my other three brothers. A part of me died when he died.

"Yes. It's time. I miss them." She doesn't continue to question me. If she wants to know any more than that, she doesn't ask. She knows I can't tell her anything about where I've been or what I've done. I need quiet time to myself to sort all of this out before I see her.

"And then you're mine!"

"Yep." My mind slips back to Kaleb with the word *mine*. The way he said he wanted me to be his and the way he has a way of claiming me every time we're together frustrates me. This trip will do me good.

"Hey. How do you feel about Alabama?"

I ask, quickly pulling my thoughts from everything Kaleb. I can't think about him right now. The need to get my life back on track has to come before him, or any man for that matter.

"Is this a trick question?"

"No. One of the Captains from my team invited me to his ranch for a few days. How does a road trip sound?"

"It sounds damn perfect. I think it's exactly what I need!"

"Alright, get packed up, we're leaving Friday, so I'll let you know more details after I talk to Harris."

"Oh, he sounds cute."

"What makes you think it's a guy?"

"Because I'm your only female friend, Jade. We both know you roll with men better than women in the grand scheme of life." She's right. Shit, I can't think of any other woman I've actually remained friends with over the years. We just generally don't have much in common. Partly due to the fact I'm a soldier and most of them are wives of soldiers. I don't really know why, but she's right.

"I'll let you decide that for yourself. I'll see you after I go see my parents, then we'll talk more. If it goes well, I'll stay with them, if not I'll be home sooner." God, I need to talk to them. I know things will be awkward with the way I left. I know without a doubt that my parents love me, they love us all. It's me who is dealing with more guilt than I'm willing to carry anymore. It's time I at least attempt to be strong enough to handle the look on my mom's face when she speaks of him. The elicit effect from what I'd done triggered my stubbornness into reality. I should've been there for him. I owe my parents the respect they deserve. I owe them the right to see their daughter.

"Jade, I'm so excited that you're home, but I hope it goes well and I don't see you for a few more days." Her attitude turns serious.

"I know. Me too." I'm not excited about anything, but I have to fake it. I am hopeful though. I'm hopeful I can make amends with a few things in my life. My parents are the first step to being successful in that.

"See you soon!" She hangs up, and I take some time before I call Harris. I think a trip like this is exactly what I need. I'm just not sure it should be with him. Who knows what Kaleb has said to him; and I can only imagine the shit going through Harris' head. Well, there's one thing I know for sure, Harris will say what's on his mind. He won't sit on anything too long, so I know if something did go on between the two of them, he'll tell me.

"Shit." His phone goes directly to voicemail. He's probably either sleeping or fucking someone, who the hell knows with him. I hope he's done both; he deserves both after what we've been through. I leave him a message, letting him know I'd love to join him for that road trip and that I'm bringing Mallory. Also, that I'm at my parents' for a few days, he can text me the time and the directions.

By the time I hang up, I'm pulling down the old, familiar street. Everything looks the same as it did all those years I lived here. Flowers are blooming and the grass is green. My heart literally leaps from the thought of seeing my parents. The white house with the big backyard looks the same. Except for the swing on the front porch and a few potted plants on the steps, it's exactly as I remember.

"Jade. Oh my goodness." My mom exits the house before I'm all the way out of the car. I pause for a moment and just take her in. She looks beautiful. Her blond hair is now streaked with silver, but her skin is still flawless. She has aged hardly at all.

"Mom." Slamming the door to my car, I run to her. Her arms encircle me the moment I hit the top step. I don't care what anyone says, there's nothing like being in the arms of your mom. I suck in a sharp breath; she smells the same. Like cookies and vanilla. A weird combination, I know, but my mom always made cookies. She always tucked a few extra away for me to eat with her; with four brothers and my dad she had to.

"You look tired, honey. Come in. Your father is in the back." I am tired, both physically and mentally, and being here causes an emotional pull I'm just not sure I should've rushed. It's great right here on the porch. I'm just teetering on the edge of jumping into the past. A past I walked away from knowing it was the best thing to do at the time. She lays her soft hand on my arm and lightly encourages me through the front door.

I smile when we step inside. The same photographs of me and all my siblings still fill the one wall. The same exact leather furniture sits next to my dad's ratted recliner, which is still in the spot directly in front of the television. These are the signs that I know I'm home.

I don't have time to reminisce long before my mom makes my presence known to my dad. "Christopher! Look who's here!" She yells out to the man who is sitting in the sunroom watching a ball game from the sounds of the loud play-by-play announcements over his speakers.

"You have got to be shitting me? My girl! Well damn, it's about time you pulled your head out of your ass and brought it home. Get in here and have a beer with your old man. The Marlins are playing, up 3-0 in the bottom of the third." Some things never change. This is why I needed to come home. I needed to see they were alright. I won't lie and say the guilt of staying away hasn't been eating at me.

I sit softly on the edge of the couch near my dad and face the game, hoping he'll continue to allow this whole thing to not be a terrible idea. Coming home should not feel like I'm walking on eggshells, but it does. "I know you can't talk about what's bothering you, Jade, just know this will always be your home. We'll always be your parents." My mom sits next to me, and we both sit back to relax against the back of the couch. I feel my body loosen up slightly. We sit like this for an entire inning and listen to my dad yell at the umpires for every bad call that's made. He's always been an avid Marlin fan.

I watch him. He has aged some since I left. Gray covers his head, and the rough stubble on his face excels with age as well. He's still strikingly handsome, in shape, and the best dad a girl could ask for.

He eventually leans in closer to me and asks why I haven't called home. I've had my feet tucked under me, watching him and the game in silence, but his words snap me upright, and tears instantly well in my eyes.

"I'm sorry, dad, mom." I shift my head to look at her. "I should've called. I just...."

"We're sorry too, honey. We're all to blame for the past few years, and I won't have you taking all the blame. You need to know that your dad and I are very proud of you." Her words cause more tears to fall, and I just watch as she stands to say what she's obviously been thinking about saying as we sat there without a word between us all. She walks closer to me and stands face-to-face as she continues softly.

"Look at what you've done with your life. You set out as a child to fulfill a dream, and you have succeeded. How can any two parents who love their daughter as much as we do not be proud of that?" My mom looks me in the eyes and smiles. Her smile is genuine and kind. It's the greatest thing I've seen in a long time, and her words mean more than she'll ever know.

"It's true. Hell, I brag about you all the time to the guys at the restaurant. Every morning over coffee and those chocolate-covered glazed donuts you used to love. None of the bastards have a thing on my ass. My daughter's in The Special Forces."

"You've followed my career," I say, stunned as I watch my father stand as well.

"Of course we have. Shit, Jade. We love you so much. I don't want us to dwell on the past. Not with the future that lies ahead of us, and not with these Marlins kicking some ass today." I run my finger down the condensation on the glass bottle of my beer, hiding the laugh or the rest of the tears that want to burst out of me.

My mom wraps her arms around me and pulls me back toward the couch. We sit and enjoy the game for a few more minutes before she asks who needs another beer. I follow her to the kitchen, while my father stays behind. "Maybe we can spend a day together soon, just the two of us women." She's smiling the largest smile I can imagine from her. She looks truly at peace and happy right now, and I wonder how she hides it so well. She has to hurt still, because I do.

"I'd like that, mom." I sit on the bar stool and watch as she wipes down every already clean counter and wrings out the rag in the sink.

"We could go shopping. Do you know how long it's been since I've bought clothes for myself?" I can only imagine. She never was one to fuss over herself. She raised all of us kids, making sure we had what we needed before she even thought of spending a dime on herself. Of course, my father came before her as well.

"Only if you let me treat you."

"Nonsense, Jade. Honestly, I just want to know that you're ok. You don't know how many times I've practiced what I'd say to you if I ever had the chance."

"Mom. I know." She has to know I've thought the same way. The way our last conversation ended had me dreading this, and I'm not too sure the years away weren't exactly what we all needed. Jason never would've suggested it, but he didn't really have that choice.

"I went to his grave before I stopped here." She stops moving and stands with her back to me.

"I go every single day."

"I figured you did." She starts to retrace her pattern on the counters, it's how she deals with pain; she cleans and stays distracted as if it'll all go away if she never stops.

"Just tell me you won't follow in his footsteps all the way to the end, Jade. I just can't take it again." Her words choke me up, and I struggle to get my own past the huge lump in my throat.

"Mom, I won't. I promise." My words are a promise I fully plan to keep, but we both know the casualties of this career aren't always during a war on enemy territory. Sometimes the worst war is the one we have in our heads after we come back home. My brother battled with a decision he made for about six months before he chose to end the fight.

"Please just give me this, Jade, tell me you'll come to me before it gets that bad. Tell me you'll let me help you if you ever think like that. I can't bury a second child. It's your job to bury me." I know where she's coming from. I watch her through my own tears again and nod my head as soon as she finally looks up at me through her own. She sees my pain. I know she does, and the strength behind her hug when she wraps me up again in her arms tells me just that.

"Now that's enough crying. This is supposed to be a happy time. We should go to dinner or something. Let me call your brothers and see if they can make it in tonight."

"Mom, can we just stay in? You can tell them tomorrow I'm back and plan something next week. I just really want to spend time with you and dad right now." She smiles and moves to the refrigerator. She begins to talk as she pulls things out of the freezer for dinner.

"How does steak sound?"

"Perfect. I think I'm going to take a long, hot shower if you don't mind."

"Of course, Jade. You know where your room is." I slide off the bar stool and move down the hall, closing my eyes tightly as I pass Jason's room, swallowing the memories flooding my head as I do. It's strange to feel the strong pull to his room when I pass, but I know I'm not ready for that.

I let the hot water burn my skin and make the hurt inside dissipate just slightly as it does. I wish more than anything that I could talk to Jason right now about where my head is at. He would understand more than anyone; he's lived it. He knows what it's like to kill a child; after all, it consumed him for the last months of his life as he tried to overcome it and failed.

CHAPTER TWELVE
JADE

Three beers and a few chocolate chip cookies down, and a breakfast date arranged with my dad before the night ends, give me a good feeling with both of my parents. A shower that lasted a half hour was exactly what I needed despite the soreness still in my arm. I have my mom help me wrap it, and I'm very proud of her for not asking any questions she knows I won't be able to answer. It's not an obvious bullet graze, but it is apparent I was hurt out there. I just wish the true ache in my head would disappear and the heaviness I'm carrying around in my heart would go away by the time this wound heals.

I'm climbing into my old twin bed, ready to succumb to sleep, when my text messages go off. Harris is finally getting back with me, and before I have the chance to reply to his second text, he's calling me.

No *'Hello Jade, how are you feeling?'* Just good ole Harris getting straight to the point.

To be honest, I'm thankful he isn't trying to coddle me. Or become all possessive. I'm even more grateful we didn't cross over that unwritten line of friendship. We came damn close, too close actually. It may have ruined the friendship I cherish too much and made things awkward.

"Do you want me to pick you both up on Friday?" he offers, and honestly, the thought of him dealing with most of the driving sounds nice. Mallory and I won't be able to cut completely loose, but I'm sure they'll get along well enough to make the weekend trip.

"Sure. What exactly are your plans for Alabama, Harris?"

"Absolutely fucking nothing. I want to just be free in the damn US of A for a damn minute without an itinerary or schedule to follow."

"Sounds damn perfect. What time do you plan to head out?"

"I'll head your way that morning, so say... around three o'clock I'll be by to get you both."

"We'll be packed."

"Hey." The line goes silent as I wait for him to continue.

"Yeah."

"You okay?" His voice is truly sincere, and I can feel his warmth through the phone. Well, there goes that thought from moments ago. He means well. I know he does. I'll touch lightly on the subject with him. I will be okay and his concern warms me. I've been entirely wrapped up in my career for so long that for once I need to put myself first, especially now that I'm home where I can deal with this my own way. Because when you're out there fighting, it's not only you, it's an entire team. We all depend on each other.

"I'm working on it." He knows it, there's no use hiding it from him. This man has been my shadow and vice versa for months. When you work that closely with someone, you get to know what they're thinking and feeling. Plus, I'm sure my situation in itself warrants his concern.

"Alright. I'll talk to you Friday. Bring your shit kickers, you're going to need them."

"I don't own shit kickers, Harris." I should've known his country ass would have me doing some insane stuff that will most likely involve us getting into shit. Literally.

"Go buy some." He hangs up. Fucker. Shit kickers, my ass. I place my phone back on the nightstand and connect it to my charger before I switch off the light. Every part of my body is physically and mentally drained to the point that I don't remember a damn thing after I roll over onto my side and sleep for eight hours straight for the first time in at least a month.

"Alright, you win. I'll take the box of donuts and dinner next week at your favorite Irish Pub, dad. You do know though I'm going to have to work out extra hard for eating these donuts." The way he looks at me, and his damn eye is twitching, I know he's coming back with a smartass comment.

"Do me a favor and use those muscles you have to knock your brother Jeremy in the water. He's still cocky as hell. A good ass-whooping is what he needs." I slide the box of donuts and my small bag into the back seat of my car, laughing. Jeremy will never change. His mouth has gotten him into more trouble than any other person I know.

"I'll do my best. Maybe pay him back for all the things he did while we were growing up. Thanks for everything, dad," I say seriously.

"Anything for you, Jade. You have a great time this weekend." He pulls me into his arms. I could stay wrapped up in him forever, but I need to go. I've had a great time with my parents these last few days. Shopping with my mom, lunch and a much needed mani/pedi, which will probably be ruined by the time Harris has me cleaning up pig shit with these damn shit kickers I have on my feet. These things are hideous. It should be fun though; laughing is exactly what I need.

My idea of fun is not rolling around in shit, but hey, after talking to my doctor on the phone yesterday and getting clearance to go back to active duty when I'm called, I probably should live a little and experience things outside of work before I'm back at it. I worked really hard to make the doctor believe I was ok. Deep down I'm dealing with it, but it's something I need to work out on my own. A trip like this will give me more time to process it all.

"Drive safe, baby girl." After pulling away from dad, I'm enthralled by my mom's arms. A tear escapes my eye by the time she lets me go. This time, it's a happy tear.

I enjoy the drive to my apartment and take the time to reflect on everything that's been heavy on my shoulders. Killing that child. Kaleb. Jason. My parents. It truly feels great to have at least one area of my life taken care of somewhat, but the others are enough to cause my gut to wrench in pain just thinking about them. I wonder if Kaleb is extremely pissed that I left him like I did. One day, I'll find him and apologize. I think he'll understand I needed me time to process my living nightmare.

"Well, fuck me. Is that really my roommate? My best friend?" Mallory damn near mauls my ass when I step through the door of our apartment.

"I should be the one asking you that. You dyed your hair. Shit, Mallory. I love it. It brings out the green in your eyes." Damn, she looks great. Her normal long, blond hair is dark brown, framing her face.

"I do too. I needed a change. You look good too, and you have about fifteen minutes to pack before this friend of yours shows up. He better be as hot as you say he is or I'll personally kick your ass. Nice boots by the way." Harris texted me earlier this morning, stating he would pick us up around one o'clock. It's a little over a six-hour drive to get to Sterett, Alabama, where his ranch is.

"Did you pack yours?" I reply sarcastically, knowing damn well she did. She may be from the city, but I can't count the times she's talked me into going to a country bar so she can line dance while I sit and laugh my ass off at the way she shakes her ass on that floor.

"Dumb question. Now go pack. I'm thirsty for a good throttle from a cowboy. Do you think he has a whip?" Her eyes light up when she asks that. Christ. I hope she's joking. Well, maybe not. The thought of her and Harris hooking up would be great for the two of them. It might even keep him occupied, get his mind off of drilling me about Kaleb Maverick. I inwardly sigh, knowing damn well whether they hook up or not, he's going to want answers. Answers I can't give him, because hell, I don't even know myself. I can't count the times I've picked up my phone over the past few days to call him just to hear his voice, only to toss my phone aside. A part of me wants to wait and see if he will reach out to me, to know if the things he said to me were true, if he wants to try and make this work, while the other part of me is scared out of my mind.

"I'm sure he has anything you need, Mal. Just don't break his heart," I tease and saunter into my room. It looks exactly the way I left it. Except for the suitcase on top of the bed Mallory must have retrieved out of my closet. I drop my bag on the floor and make my way to my closet, pulling down a few sleeveless shirts and bending down to grab my favorite pair of pink Converse that are battered and worn. No way in hell am I spending the entire weekend in these damn boots. After grabbing a few pair of shorts and my favorite matching lace bra and panties along with the rest of the things I need, I'm packed and ready to go, just in time for the doorbell to ring.

"Hey. You must be Mallory?" I hear Harris' deep voice ask.

"Um. I am. Harris, right?" I wait just inside my bedroom door. My hand flies to my mouth to stifle my laugh. I warned her he was hot. Now, for the first time since I've known her, she's flustered. I can tell by the tone of her voice.

"It's Beau actually. Everyone in the Army calls me Harris. You ladies ready?" Damn, Harris. I can feel his smoothness through these walls.

"All set." I walk out of my room, towing my suitcase behind me. Mal turns around to face me, her mouth hitting the floor. Yeah, he got to her.

"Jesus Christ. You look, well fuck. You look totally different, Elliott. You clean up good."

"You do too, cowboy. Let's hit the road. My shit-kickers are ready for some shit." I lift my leg to show off my nice, new, ugly boots.

"I'll have you both pros at shoveling horse shit by the end of the weekend," he remarks, taking my suitcase from my hand and grabbing the handle of Mal's.

"After you," he says all gentleman-like. I roll my eyes when he tilts his head to the side and stares at Mal's ass in her tight short-shorts when she walks by.

"Pervert," I whisper.

"She has a nice ass. What the fuck can I say?" He shrugs.

"Say whatever you want. Just gag her, she's a screamer." I nudge him. She's not a screamer. More like a moaner. I'm not going to tell him any differently though.

Setting our alarm and locking up behind me, I follow them down the corridor and onto the sidewalk only to come to a screeching halt when he stops by the biggest black truck I have ever seen. Maybe I don't know this man like I thought I did. This is a country boy's truck for damn sure.

"Don't say a damn thing, Elliott. Trust me, I would much rather be in my Mustang," he says when he notices the shocked expression on my face.

"Whatever you say, cowboy."

"And knock it off with the cowboy shit." He raises his brows, and I burst out laughing. God, it feels good to laugh. The smile on my face fades when I see the Jeep parked on the street right in front of my house. It's Kaleb. I'd recognize that Jeep anywhere.

I don't waste any time marching straight to his door, yanking it open, and unleashing on him. "So now you're fucking stalking me? Kaleb, you have to learn fucking boundaries. You can't just show up in front of my house and watch me. You don't think I'll see your goddamn Jeep when you park directly in front of my house?" He has already stepped out of his Jeep and slammed the door. He has turned so that my back is against the side of the truck, and fuck if he hasn't already smashed his hard body against mine. My deep breaths hit him in the face as he just watches me closely.

"What were you saying?" Fuck if I know, because when he's near me, I can't do logic, especially when he's this close. My mind starts the insanity of wanting to touch him even though the reason I'm over here is to tell his ass off.

"I was saying.... You can't just watch me."

"Oh, but Jade. Watching you is exactly what I want to do. Your perfect skin..." He moves his hand down my arm, sending chills all over my body. How does he do this to me? My mind was so clear from the few days at my parents' house, now I can't even put him in his fucking place.

Our eyes are locked. His other hand begins to slide down my other arm, skipping slightly as he covers my wrap. I let my eyes fall to his chest and watch as it rises with each breath he takes.

I swallow hard and finally speak. "It's fucked up, Kaleb. I can't deal with fucked up. I need something normal. I don't want to worry that you're tracking me and watching my every fucking move." A smirk lands on his face, and I watch him contemplate his next sentence.

"Jade, I was simply stopping by to check on you. That is it. I haven't heard from you since you ran from my bed. I know you have shit you're dealing with, and I'm just worried about you. But if I ever wanted to track you, I could."

"I know you could, and I don't want that shit in my life. If we're going to see each other at all, you have to leave the technology to the level of normal people, Kaleb. I'm not kidding. A cell phone or email, that's it."

"So we're *seeing* each other?" He backs off just slightly, still pressed up against me, just not as tightly.

"I didn't say that. I'm just laying down the ground work if we're going to consider it. Even if we're just friends, I need boundaries and you.... You don't seem to have any of those."

"You have no idea the restraint I have with you, my sweet Jade. I can deal with your rules, but you need to deal with mine." My eyes move to his again, and I wait for him to continue. "You can't fucking run. You want normal... Then you have to communicate like normal, and when I want to taste your fucking body, you let me. Because remember, Jade, I want you. I can deal with your rules outside the bedroom, but I make the rules inside. Beyond that, I don't give two fucks how we set it up. I just want to know you're on the same page as me."

I don't know if we're on the same page or not completely, but I nod in agreement, because honestly, my body wouldn't allow any other reply.

His mouth lands on mine, and his arms pull me closer to him, even though that didn't seem possible in the moments before. His kiss is passionate, and I find myself matching his intensity. He feels good and wrong at the same time. Like I'm playing with an explosive that will go off any second. Of course, it could simply be the fact that Harris is nearby and has to be seeing all of this. Shit.

I push Kaleb off of me and breathe deeply, pulling my thoughts together. What am I doing? Do I want this with Kaleb? Yes. Do I want to deal with the pissing contest between the two of them? No.

I look over and see Mallory smiling the biggest damn smile of her life, while Harris is loading the back of his truck with harsh movements. I know he's pissed about this, but he's going to have to get over it.

"Were you going away with Harris?" Kaleb's face has dropped, and it's obvious he truly wasn't watching us before. If he would've seen all the luggage and us walking out together, our conversation would've been so much worse.

"My friend Mallory and I were going to meet him in Alabama, but he offered to drive us instead. It's just a weekend away that I desperately need. Nothing more, Kaleb."

"I bet he did."

"Stop. I'm not dealing with that either. I've told you we are nothing more than friends, I need you to own that."

"I've seen you with him, Jade. It's hard for me to not want to kill him." Yeah, well, it's hard for me to not want to kill you right now. I don't say that. But I sure as hell feel it. What I do say is what he needs to hear.

"He also went to battle with you and had your back the whole damn time. This will be a deal breaker with me. You two have to get along."

"Fucking hell, Jade. He would fuck you right now if you offered."

"He's a guy, of course he would. I'm not talking about this again, so you need to deal with it. I've told you we are nothing more than friends and that's the truth." I watch him watch Harris. He's glaring at him, and right now, I wish I could go back in time and not meet Kaleb the same way. Being wrapped around Harris probably wasn't the best first impression I could give, but it is what it is. That's how it happened, and it's what probably sparked Kaleb to go after me like he did in the first place.

"I'll deal with it." The muscle in his jaw moves as he tightens it.

"Yes, you will. Right now." I wanted to make amends with things in my past, but I need to do it with my present as well. These two guys need to know where I stand, and I can't think of a better time than right now. "Follow me."

I walk away, leaving him no chance to react, then walk up to Harris and tell him we all need to sort this shit out. "Let's talk inside." Mallory looks entirely confused, however, she follows us in instead of pumping me full of questions outside. I know she's biting her damn tongue.

Once we get inside, I let it all out. "Harris, I'm seeing Maverick. Kaleb, I'm not seeing Harris. You two have to stop with the alpha bullshit and let me breathe before I kill you both. Harris, you know I love you, but it was never more than friends even though we almost crossed that line. It would've never been more than a fuck. I want to see what Kaleb and I have beyond the insanely great sex. I deserve this. I want to see where it goes, but I need you two to stop. This isn't helping any of us. In fact, it's driving me crazy. It ends now." Kaleb's fucking smirk spreads across his lips, while Harris looks as confused as ever.

"Who the fuck is Maverick?" Mallory's voice pulls me into a smile. How comical this shit must look to her. I've never been in a relationship before, and now there are two men in our apartment. This whole scenario is new to her, so I can only imagine what she's thinking.

I point to Kaleb. "He's Maverick."

"You people and your using last names crap. How can I keep up? Nice to meet you, Maverick, Kaleb... Whatever your name is." She moves forward to shake his hand. "I'm Mallory, her best friend, who knows absolutely nothing about you or the shit she just spewed, but you better know I will be drilling her very soon."

"Drill away." He doesn't even bother to hide his arrogance. The damn bastard is so confident. The way he stands there with his arms crossed around his massive chest and those tattoos daring me to come and lick them. Ugh.

"And you almost fucked this one? Damn it, Jade. Crush a girl's heart, why don't you?" Harris looks at Mallory but still hasn't moved from his spot. He's processing all of this, and I can see his wheels turning. He's about to let loose what he's thinking.

"Just like I told him before, if he lays one fucking mark on you, I'll kill him. I know we're never going to be more than what we already are... But that's the reason I'll never let any man hurt you. It's that code we live by. We protect our team. Jade, you're a part of my team forever, and I would die making sure you're safe." He ends his words staring right at Kaleb. Kaleb stares back, and I watch the two of them exchange so many things without a single word leaving either of their mouths.

"Do you two need to beat the shit out of each other and battle this out, or should you just whip your dicks out and measure?

Better yet, we can have you stand side by side and see who can piss the farthest. I'll let Jade judge the piss, and I can always judge the size. I mean, boys, we can work this out." Mallory stands next to them both, looking up and instantly softening both of their demeanors. They look down at her and smile. I laugh out loud at her craziness, and then she continues. "What you need to do is invite him to Alabama. Give Jade the chance to see where this is going for her, while you get the benefit of watching him close on your own terms." She points and touches Harris' arm with the tip of her finger. "Damn, that's hard. Okay... Stay focused, Mal. And you, Mr. Maverick. You need to remember it will be me first you have to deal with if she's so much as crying over you, then I'll let this big gorilla over here at you if there's anything left." Both men turn to look at me as she continues to talk. Their faces are amused, and her tiny frame walking in front of them both, taking charge, is a sight I needed to see. This is damn hysterical.

"I'd poke your arm too, but I don't think I can handle that again. A woman can only take so much sexy as all hell men in her apartment, especially when they look like the two of you, and trust me, I mean that in a very good way. Now, let's all play nice, get our asses in that truck, and burn up the road. Okay, boys? This girl is using her vacation days on a road trip with her best friend. We were supposed to be Thelma and Louise—without jumping off the cliff at the end, of course. Now we have so much testosterone, I'm not sure we'll even get to where we're going." She walks toward the door, hoping they'll follow, but they don't right away.

"Maverick. You're more than welcome to go with us to my ranch in Alabama for the weekend. I have plenty of room at the ranch house." Harris follows Mallory out the door, and I don't miss his smile when she passes in front of him.

Kaleb and I are left alone in the house. I want to know what he's thinking, but won't ask. Instead I say, "So what do you say? Feel like going to Alabama?"

CHAPTER THIRTEEN
KALEB

Hell, yes, I want to go to Alabama with her. I want nothing more than to spend time with her away from all of the stress we're dealing with, but I have a job. The orders came in this morning, and it's something that needs to be done now. It won't take more than a day, but I have to handle it myself. In all honestly, I should've done it before I ever drove to see her, but I had reached my limit of not knowing how she was doing.

"I'd love to meet you there. I can be there tomorrow." Her smile falters just slightly, but she attempts to hide it. I like that she wants me to come with her, and it just sends a fire inside me to get there even sooner. She's so fucking beautiful. I thought that in the pictures, which were no comparison to her in the desert and now seeing her in civilian clothes with her hair down, which makes me just want to wrap my hands into that hair. She's wearing more makeup than usual, which I could go either way with. She has a natural beauty that doesn't need enhanced as far as I'm concerned.

"Okay. I'll send you the exact address and you can come later." I move in on her as she starts to talk. She's mine. She just made it official, and I want to take her into my arms and celebrate the best way we know how, but that'll have to wait. Her slight smile has me hopeful that this trip will be the breakthrough we both need. And Christ, she looks so much better than the last time I saw her. Her color is back. Her spark that drives me crazy, even her attitude is different. Everything about her strikes me straight to my chest.

"I'll be there as soon as I finish up some loose ends... And then I'm all yours." Pulling her closely against my body reminds me of how perfectly we fit together.

"I'll be waiting!" She seems relaxed and at peace in this moment. I can't help but notice her arms around my waist, sliding lower until her hands are full of my ass cheeks. She gives them a squeeze, then kisses me on the lips before she pulls away. "I'd better get out there." Her beautiful eyes light up when she speaks.

"I have to go anyway. I'll see you soon." I lay my forehead against hers for a mere second, then kiss that same spot.

We both walk outside, and I watch her get into the truck before I get into my driver's seat. She's so different here at home now that she's had a few days to herself. I had no idea how much I'd love that.

They pull away, and I'm not a block down the road before she sends me a text with the address of his ranch. I feel the adrenaline begin to surface with the thought of what this weekend could bring for us. It should be a great time, and I'm hoping that firecracker Mallory keeps Harris busy.

Seeing her tell him in person is really the best gift she could've given me. I wanted him to know that what I told him on the airplane wasn't me just being delusional. She said it with her own mouth now, so he will respect that. He is a man of honor and respect; even though we haven't seen eye-to-eye on Jade, I get where he's coming from.

I'm glad she has someone like that to watch over her, even though he won't need to do that any longer.

I drive the few hours thinking about her. Once I pull in at the office, I see Kase's truck is here, so I know I'm late to our meeting. He's already turned everything on by the time I'm through the doors. Our technology is highly secured and top of the line. It has to be for what we use it for. "What's the status?" I ask, then grab a chair, flipping it around to straddle it. My hands rest on the top.

"Intel shows Al-Quaren is moving through Mexico. We're going to have to be ready to move."

"Goddamn Mexico. I hate going in there to find someone. Why can't these assholes stay where their native land is?"

"I know. We have informants there though, so he'll settle in, and we'll go in and pull his ass out of his hole."

"These guys think they're men hiding in a shithole to avoid their death. What happened to facing it like a man? No, they send out their babies to do that." I pause, thinking about Jade and her face as she pulled the trigger. I knew the minute she pulled the trigger it would haunt her, and I will forever owe her for that shot.

"I do know there are four men with him. They're all dressing alike, so it's hard to tell which one is Al-Quaren. We're going to have to check his markings to confirm."

"What time is this conference?" I'm getting impatient, knowing getting him is going to be a struggle. He's been on our radar for years and right now, I'm down two men who are working in Iraq on another project.

"They will be dialing in shortly." The computer begins to ring, and we wait while The President of the United States starts to talk to us both. His face comes across the screen. The deep circles under his eyes let me know this isn't coming lightly. Christ. I could never run a country. Every president in office has always had my respect. The day-to-day struggles they all deal with would put most of us in a mental hospital. I listen intently as he starts to speak. His words come out strong and very demanding.

"Thank you for meeting with me on this. I'm calling in your help, because I know your history of success in taking out international terrorists. I want this guy captured and brought in for questioning. He has vital information about national security we need to get our hands on. I'll use the most effective ways to interrogate him to get that information, but first I need to find him. That's where you two come in." We both watch, knowing we'll be going in. Our men are the best of the best, and I have no problem organizing another team like the last one to smoke him out.

"He's working with a Mexican cartel and will be tough to pull out of there. Tell me what you need, and I'll get you the resources." He turns to talk to someone on his right, then quickly back to us.

"This time I can't offer you any soldiers. This needs to be done completely with your men."

"Sir, I'd like you to reconsider. I need a sniper and a point man to fill my team. I'd like to request two of the soldiers that just completed the mission I was on last week. They are brilliant in their positions and would be exactly what I need to get in and out successfully."

"Resources I can do. Who are the two you have specifically in mind?"

"Captain Elliott and Captain Harris of the US Army."

"I'll grant you two soldiers for this mission, but they'll need to agree to go AWOL before I can approve this. I want zero connections with the US Army in the event your mission is compromised. I'll have half of your funds moved soon, so they're there for you to fulfil the job. Once it's finished, the rest of the money will be transferred." All of this is the normal agreement I have to make when I get a call. This is just the first that came directly from The President.

"When do you want us to go in?" Kase asks.

"One week. He's been staying at his locations for about two weeks before he moves. He's just changed locations, so we'll get you down there once we get his location verified, then send your team in before he moves out." I sit still and watch The President give us orders, knowing this is a huge mission for us. I also know it's a very dangerous one and one I'll be very ready to have behind me. I'm not completely familiar with the area of Mexico that he's been in, and I'm going to have to do thorough research before I leave for this.

I know I'll only have a few days with Jade before I have to leave for the compound in Missouri. The team will have to meet me there for briefing before we leave out.

"My team will be in touch before the mission. Do me proud, Maverick. I need this guy alive, and I need you to deliver him to me without an audience. Go in there without any markings and get out quick." He's saying everything I already know. It's why we're the elite group of men who get called for the most dangerous jobs in the world. The military uses us when they want to stay hidden and stay off the radar. An invasion like this could cause a huge war we aren't ready to fight. I know as well as he does if we get caught out there, we're on our own. The US military won't come rescue us, and we would be thrown under the bus before The President would take any heat on his own ass for this mission. It's how it works. Keep him looking as clean as possible while we do the dirty work and take all the risks. It's what I'm great at. It's what my men strive for, and we will be successful in this mission or die trying.

"Most definitely, Mr. President. We'll be in touch." Kase shuts down the technology the second we're disconnected from the live feed. We both look at each other and start planning our mission. It's hard to know everything we'll need, but one thing is certain. We need cover while we're there.

"I'll work on getting us into Mexico safe and find us a place to go. This will be tricky with all of us, but I'm thinking we'll all fly in separately. I'll check out contacts to see what I can make happen and feed you the information as it comes in." He's great at this shit. I have full faith in him.

"I have a trip I need to make for the next couple of days. I'll work through the night on anything I need to do. We'll use the burn phones to talk while I'm gone."

"Sounds good. Where you headed?"

"Alabama. I'll go to the compound from there." I stand to grab everything I'll need. Kase helps me load my Jeep without asking any more questions about where or why I'm taking off to Alabama.

Thank Christ. I'm not prepared to go into details with him yet. Once I'm settled behind my wheel, I'm off before I have a chance to grasp what I've just agreed to. I'm taking Jade to Mexico on one of the most dangerous missions I've ever considered. I know she can handle herself, but can I handle myself if anything happens to her?

I move quickly through my house to get enough clothes for the next few weeks. Leaving the door locked and a few lights on, I shut the door and begin another journey to yet another mission, but first I need to spend time with Jade.

The drive to the ranch is long, but it gives me time to think. I'm glad I got out of there quicker than I thought and get to spend more time with her out of our element. We both need this, and I can't wait to see what it does for us.

I pull in the drive and text Harris that I'm here. He's at the door before I finish the text, probably wondering who the hell is driving up this late at night. It's black out here with only a sliver of the moon shining in the cloudy sky.

I've had a long day and am looking forward to hitting a bed somewhere with Jade in my arms.

"She's in bed already. You want to have a beer with me out on the back porch?" he offers, and I decide to accept. This man is extremely good at what he does and for that I have to respect him.

He hands me the beer, and we both sit on a wooden deck with a fire pit burning. I can only imagine the conversations that could happen at a setup like this. "I received a call today that you'd be talking to me. I can only assume you want me on a mission."

"Yes. That's right. You and Jade both. It's in Mexico. A terrorist we've been after for years. You'd have to take a temporary walk until we got back. Going AWOL was mentioned." I can feel the heat of his anger over the blaring fire. He's pissed about going AWOL, and I don't blame the man at all.

"You expect me to literally walk away from everything I've worked my life for to work on your team. When I honestly have thought of exactly how I'd kill you if you hurt Jade."

"That is actually how I know you're perfect. You and I may not agree on everything, but we both want her safe."

"I'm not too sure I'd consider putting her on a mission like this as *keeping her safe*. It's actually more of a death mission, if you ask me."

"It's a dangerous mission I know she can handle, just as we both can. My team of men will also do great in Mexico."

"But I have to walk away from the Army to help you. Why would I ever do that?"

"To keep your country safe. To take down one of the most disgusting human beings on the planet. To walk beside Jade, because you know she'll be in."

"Good points. Can I have your word that we're good? I can't worry about my fucking back out there."

"I'd never take a personal issue on a mission. We have an understanding as far as I'm concerned. You know Jade is mine, and I'll understand that you have a spot in her life that won't cross any lines."

"She made it very clear today that she's worried about trying this with you, but also talked about how she hopes you two can coexist out here." Well fuck, next to hearing her finally admit she wants to see what we can build together, that's the best goddamn news I've heard.

"I can understand that. It's chaos for a person to come and go in the military. We may both eventually go separate ways, but it doesn't hurt to make the best of the time we have together now. However, I'm not planning on going anywhere. I care about her, I really do."

"I agree. And for what it's worth, I believe you." I don't respond to that. In fact, the silence becomes lighter as we both take big swigs of our beers. He tosses the cap into the fire, and I watch the flame as he continues to talk.

"The next few days will be mission-free. I want zero agendas. I want no schedule, and I plan to take each moment for what it is. I need relaxation, and this looks like it will be all I have before I walk away from my career to help you."

"This wouldn't be happening if you weren't the best." That's the fucking truth. Harris and I may have started out on opposite sides, but this man knows his shit. And he'll respect the boundaries. He's proven that. I respect the man more for having this talk with me and for not being afraid to tell me how he feels.

"I know." I stand. I need to go to bed, and it's time to hold my girl. My girl. I really like the sound of that.

"She's down the hall, second door on the right."

"Good night, Harris." I pick up my bag as I pass back through the main entry and open the door to her room quietly. There's a dim nightlight, allowing me to see her on the bed. I move slowly, trying hard not to wake her. Slipping off my shoes and jeans, I finish dropping all of my clothes on my side of the bed. Right before I reach for the covers, she begins to stir.

Her movements become faster and her moans louder. It's as if she's saying 'no' over and over. I know better than to climb in bed with a soldier during a nightmare, so I sit on the edge of the bed and try talking to her. She doesn't snap out of it and only becomes louder. Her face is scrunched up, and I reach to touch her head in hopes of pulling her out of it. She screams just as I touch her. Her eyes fly open, and she jumps up from her sleeping position and punches the fuck out of my back.

I stand, knowing I'm fucked because I'm butt-ass naked, praying she doesn't attack again. The door flies open, and Harris is standing in the doorway, while I'm holding my dick behind my hands. This isn't exactly how I thought this night would go.

CHAPTER FOURTEEN
JADE

My heart is racing and my adrenaline is pumped. I'm ready to kill anyone in my path as I unleash hell on my attackers. I can hear Kaleb talking in the background, and I know if I can get through this, he'll be here soon.

All of a sudden, a loud slam of the door pulls me from my apparent nightmare. I come to and see Kaleb standing naked with Harris in the room. "What the fuck did I miss?" My voice is panicky.

"You were having a nightmare," Kaleb says. His tone is worried. My body is covered in sweat, and I stand on the bed just to regain my composure of where I even am. It takes me a few moments to remember I'm at Harris' ranch and that Kaleb is here. Shit, that sounds like a real fucking nightmare. Not to mention that Kaleb is naked.

"Why aren't you wearing clothes?"

"Because I was climbing into bed with you when you started hollering. You were having a nightmare, and I value my dick enough to not go near you when you're not clear." Harris chuckles from the doorway. That shit isn't funny.

"Jade, I'm out. See you in the morning." Harris closes the door, and I close my eyes at the absurdity of this entire situation, trying to calm my beating heart.

He's still standing with both hands covering himself. My eyes travel across his chest, and I finally lie back and pat the bed next to me. He looks at me with a little uncertainty before he exposes himself to me and moves the covers to get in beside me. Damn, he's hot, even all disheveled-looking and worried.

"I sleep naked in the States," he admits.

"Of course you do." I may have had a nightmare, but I'm sure as hell alert now. Especially with him standing there gloriously naked.

"What were you dreaming about?"

"I can't remember." I truly don't remember. I've had a bad dream every night; half I remember, the other half I just wake up from with my body covered in sweat.

He slides in and drapes his arm over me before he moves even closer. I feel disgusting and quickly move to take a shower.

"I'm covered in sweat. I'm going to shower. I didn't think you'd be here until tomorrow."

"I decided to take the trip tonight." He watches me as I cross the room and move into the bathroom.

"You can join me if you feel like it!" I yell at him from the bathroom after I start the water. The shower is big enough for both of us, and if I have my way, we'll put it to great use.

He's coming through the door before I can pull my shirt off. I knew he would. If there's one thing I can say about our relationship, it's that our sexual chemistry toward one another topples anything I've experienced before. Hell, we could set a room on fire just by looking at each other.

"You sure about this, Jade? My intentions tonight were to hold you while you slept. After walking in and witnessing your nightmare—" I cut him off right there.

"I'm going to have nightmares, Kaleb. I'd give anything not to have them, but trust me, please, when I tell you I'm dealing. You know me well enough by now I hope to know that if I didn't want you in this shower with me, I would tell you. Besides, if all you do in here is hold me, then that's enough." My back is to him when I speak. I adjust the water in this huge walk-in shower.

I do turn around while I pull my tank top over my head, then I slip out of my boy shorts and walk to stand directly in front of him. Our bodies are so close, and I hunger for him to touch me.

"You'll get through it. I want you to know I'm here if you want to talk." The last thing on my mind right now is to talk. My fingers caress over his inked, tanned, toned skin.

"Someday I want you to tell me if these all have special meanings to you." I lean in and kiss the skull tattoo in the middle of his chest; it's surrounded by a set of wings so intricately designed.

"Anything you want, Jade." His eyes capture mine, his muscles flex under my touch. His cock presses against my stomach. My pussy clenches at the thought of how he feels. He has no idea, but he's exactly what I need right now. I need to feel cherished and wanted.

"Get your ass in that shower before I bend you over this sink and fuck your sweet ass again." Well damn, I was beginning to wonder when dominating Kaleb was going to come out and play.

"Yes, Sir." I smirk and drop my hands from his chest, then spin around and step into the shower, stifling back the laugh when he hisses loudly.

I lean my head back and let the hot water cascade down my back. I close my eyes briefly then snap them open when I feel him in front of me. His hands skim across my nipples, causing them to peak and scream for his attention. When he takes one in his mouth, I moan. The way he works my body sends shivers down my spine in spite of the fact we're standing in a scorching hot shower. His hand flicks and toys with one nipple, while his mouth nips at the other. "God, Kaleb." I arch into him, begging for more. He changes positions, working the other breast with his mouth, while his other hand plays with the one his mouth left. Before I can speak, I'm being hoisted up, my legs wrapped around his waist, as he steps backwards and sits on the long marbled seat. His cock is so close to where I need him to be. Where I am now beginning to believe he was meant to be.

"Ride me, baby. Wrap me in your sweetness. Take what belongs to you." His voice is gruff and full of desire.

His hands move up and down my inner thighs to the round curve of my ass, pressing his long erection into my core. The urge to have his mouth on mine while I sink down on him drives me to nip at his bottom lip. I'm desperate to let him hear what he does to me through our mouths when we connect.

When my tongue sweeps across his, our mouths open up. I lift my hips and trace my finger up the length of his cock, then grip him firmly in my hands, placing him where I want him. My greedy pussy opens up as he stretches me wide, while I moan my pleasure into his mouth, tasting his animalistic growl. God, he consumes me and fills me completely. My hands go to his head, and his hands stay on my hips, gliding me up and down so that I feel every inch of him.

Between the flush from the steam coming from the shower and my sexual desire to fulfill us both, I feel like I might melt into the damn floor at any minute.

"Fuck. You feel so good. You have no idea what you do to me. Watching you take what you want. Riding my cock. The fucked look of your wet hair and the beautiful glisten of your skin have me so hard I've got your tight pussy gripping my cock like it's so damn thirsty." His words undo me. I press him back until his head lies against the tiled wall. I ride him until my legs sting. I say his name every time he hits the spot that tempts to send me over the edge. He knows I'm close. So is he.

His lids hood over his eyes, and he lifts me, placing me up against the opposite side of the spray. He slams into me and fucks me hard. I can feel his cock pulsing and my heart screaming with the urgent need to tell him how much I want him. I need to feel the way he makes me feel; instead, I holler out his name when I feel him release inside of me. His warmth then sends me over the edge. My fingers burn from gripping his shoulders as we both come so hard our breathing is out of control.

"I'm glad you're here," I speak honestly after he pulls out of me and turns me around to stand under the hot spray. "Me too. Even though I have no fucking clue what the hell to do on a ranch."

"Me either, but getting away and spending time together is what we need. There are so many things I'm dying to know about you," I say as I reach for the soap and start to run it across his chest. I continue to clean his body from head to toe while sorting out in my head about where to start with my questions. I want to know everything about him. Our relationship started as backwards as one can get. It's time to move forward. I want to know the real Kaleb Maverick. What makes him tick? What are his likes and dislikes? What all his job entails. Everything.

"There's not much to me, Jade. What you see is what you get." He spreads his arms out wide.

"There's a lot of you to see. I want to know what's in here and here." I point to his head and his heart.

"Jade Elliott seems to be consuming both of those at the moment." He takes the soap from my hands. He returns the favor by running it carefully over my skin.

"I love that I'm there, Maverick, but tomorrow morning I want to know all about you."

"Yes, ma'am." My brows lift at those two words.

"Are we switching roles here? No more demanding Kaleb?" I tease, knowing damn well what his answer will be.

"Fuck, no. If I tell you to call me' Sir', you'll do it." I laugh and catch myself smiling long after his words.

"My hair is going to look like a frazzled mess when we get up." After drying it with a towel, brushing it out, and then putting it on top of my head in messy twist, it's going to be a nightmare. I grab my shorts and tank off of the floor, only to have them yanked out of my hands and tossed into the bedroom.

"I don't give a shit what your hair looks like, and as cute as those little items you were sleeping in are, when you sleep next to me, your fine ass is naked. Got me?" He grips my hips and starts walking us into the bedroom, while my arm flings out and catches the light switch.

"No. I don't get you. I don't mind sleeping naked, especially next to you. I can grab this anytime I want." I reach around and wrap my hand around his cock.

"Exactly my point, Jade. Now climb your ass in bed. You need rest." I won't argue with him there. I climb in, the sheets cool against my skin. Kaleb wastes no time tucking me into his side. Swinging my leg over his, I curl my arm around his waist.

"Sleep, Jade. Tomorrow we'll talk." I close my eyes. Even though I slept soundly and peacefully in my bed at my parents' house, sleeping next to Kaleb is undoubtedly the best night's sleep I've had in months.

"So let me get this straight. You left that fine piece of ass in bed to sit out here with me and have coffee? Did you fall and smack your head?" Mal reaches over, digging her fingers into my knotted-up hair.

"Quit it, you ass. And no. My head is fine. I agreed to sit out here to watch the sunrise with you and talk without any interruptions. So ask me. I know you're dying to know about him." I nudge her shoulder. We've been up for about a half hour. Last night was wonderful, getting settled in, but Mal and I really haven't had the chance to talk. She only knows what she overheard before we left. After Harris showed us around, he made a fire. We sat around and most of the conversation was directed around his ranch. I see why he loves to come here. Mal ate it up. Well, more like ate him up with her eyes. I'll definitely be touching on that subject.

"Well, where should I start? How about this. When and how long have you been fucking him?"

"A few weeks." I shrug. That was not what I expected, hell I'm not sure what I expected her to ask.

"You can't tell me shit. Can you?" She laughs.

"I can and I can't. I care about him. Everything else is complicated. You have to trust me, I guess. Trust that I'm following my heart for once, Mallory." It's the truth. I thought long and hard on the ride here yesterday. He means more to me than I was willing to admit. My mind was so consumed with what happened to me that I was willing to push him away, when in reality I need him. Not to help me continue to deal with the things I have no control over, but to make me feel for the first time in my life. To feel wanted, needed, and cherished. The way he held me all night meant just as much to me as the way he gave me space for a few days even though he really didn't want to; and the way he gave up everything without hesitation when I asked him to come here with me for the weekend. I'd be a fool to not see where we can go from here.

"Well, I'm happy for you. You deserve it, you know. Happiness and all." She takes a sip of her coffee.

"So do you. I saw the way you watched Harris' ass every time he stood up to poke the fire. I know how your mind works." I laugh freely, breathing in the fresh country air.

"Even a blind woman would want to be poked by him. Jesus. Have you looked at his ass?" I have. Time to change the subject. I'm thankful yet again nothing happened between the two of us. Whatever did happen, she doesn't mention it. What we do talk about is the visit with my parents. The dinner we have planned for the following weekend and my visit to see my brother's grave. I have no guilt left, no shame for what I did to save the man I feel I'm falling in love with and the rest of my team. The truth bears weight that if I hadn't shot that young boy, I wouldn't be sitting here with my best friend, I wouldn't be with the man who, yes, I *need* in my life. The possibility of him not being a part of my life now is undeniably not an option. I'm falling for the first time in my life, and god help me, I believe he will be there to catch me.

"Jesus Christ, that shit stinks. I could literally throw up my breakfast you gentlemen made for us this morning. That is nasty," Mallory hollers the minute we walk into the stables toward the horses. I have my shit kickers on, but I sure as hell am not shoveling shit. Thank god he was only joking about it.

His ranch is huge. He has workers who take care of his horses and their breeding. I'm more excited about riding one. And she's right about the smell being bad.

"You get used to it, and once you get out into the open field or roam around the trails, you can't smell shit out there." I love how Harris uses her words and shoves them right back in her face with a laugh. She needs it.

"Fuck Harris, these horses are beauties. Never pegged you for this." Kaleb strolls up to a reddish-colored horse that's all saddled up and ready to go. Three more of the same-colored ones are ready to go. They are breathtakingly beautiful. It's all a little intimidating, but the shiny coats are absolutely perfect.

"That's Serena. This is Tiger Lily, that one there is Diego, and the other one is Tinkerbell." He points to all of them in turn.

"Tinkerbell is for you, chicken shit." He walks over and grabs the reins, never taking his eye off of Mallory.

"I never said I was chicken." Mallory crosses her arms under her breasts. Harris' eyes divert right to them.

"Come on, mouth. I'll show you around, while these two can drift off to wherever they want." He reaches for her hand and guides her up on the horse.

"Oh shit," she squeals.

"Yeah. That's what I thought. I got you." He takes hold of her reins, heaving himself up on his horse with ease.

"You know what you're doing, Maverick?" he asks while showing Mallory how to hold the reins, pulling back slightly for the horse to stop. I'm more into watching these two interact than anything else. I've never seen her act so skittish. Either that or she's faking her damn ass off just so he'll touch her.

"Yeah, I got this." I give these two a lot of credit. What started out as a hell of a raw deal for Harris and the way Maverick has treated him, has turned into respect for one another. Over breakfast they joked around, chatted a bit. I felt comfortable for the first time around them together since they met. I was also very aware of the small glimpses of concern Harris kept shooting Maverick's way. Something else is going on. It doesn't have a thing to do with the three of us, but yet somehow it does. It's different though, like Kaleb is keeping something from me and Harris is warning him to tell me. All of my training and my gut tell me that whatever it is, I'm not going to like it at all.

"Good, just stay on the trail I told you about. You'll see the lake not too far from here. We'll meet you guys back here in a few hours."

"You ready?" Kaleb turns in my direction.

"Yes." Even though I'm nervous, I manage to get my foot in the stirrup and start to drag myself up, only to be guided by a strong pair of hands palming the curves of my ass.

"What? Those damn shorts leave nothing to my imagination. If that fine ass is going to be shoved in my face, then I'd be a damn fool not to touch it. Keep looking at me like that and I'll find something to bend you over out there and fuck that sweet ass again. This time while you scream my name." Well, shit. My legs are spread across this damn horse, making it impossible to clench them together, but my ass cheeks flex. God, that seems like forever ago.

"We'll see," I say sarcastically as I grab the reins and take charge of the horse like Harris instructed us to do over breakfast. It doesn't take Kaleb long to catch up with me as we trot side by side down the trail, taking in and enjoying the view. He pulls out of his shell and shares so much information with me about himself. He went to school in Florida and joined the Army right after high school. His father left his mother when he, a younger brother, and his sister were young.

"Your mom sounds incredible to have raised all of you by herself."

"She is. That's one of the reasons for my tattoo and why it's my favorite. She's great, so is my sister. They would love you."

"What about your brother? Are you close to him too?" I hear his breath catch. My head snaps to look at him. I'm not sure what I witness on his face; sadness, or maybe it's frustration.

"I'm not ready to talk about him. Can we leave it at that?" He looks my way. It's bitterness I see.

"Okay." That's all I manage to say. We travel in silence for a bit. He looks like he's lost in his own thoughts and memories.

I have every intention of inviting Kaleb to dinner with my family this weekend. I would love for him to meet my family before I meet his. Not sure why that's overly important to me, it just is. I blurt it out before I lose my nerve or he disappears deeper in his thoughts.

"My family is getting together for dinner Friday night. Would you like to come with me?" God, why does it feel like I'm in high school asking some guy to come and meet my parents? He stops his horse and exhales loudly.

"I can't. I won't be here. I was waiting for the right time to tell you, Jade." He looks me in the eyes. I'm not liking what I see reflecting back at me at all. I bring my horse to a stop and gather the reins, turning us both to face him.

"Is it another mission? So soon?" I swallow. Please tell me no. Tell me you're taking me to some deserted island in the middle of the Caribbean. Or to bum fuck nowhere land. Just not a mission.

"Yes. We received a call from The President himself. It's highly confidential. I thought I had a week, but I don't. Kase called me this morning, and I have to fly out Monday morning. You and Harris leave Thursday." I close my eyes as his words are sinking in. I know I'm cleared. But am I really ready for this?

"Jade." His calling of my name snaps my eyes open.

"I'm fine. I can handle it."

"I know you can. If I didn't, I wouldn't have asked you to go. That's not what I need to tell you." My brows shoot up. What the hell else is there to say?

"What?"

"Both you and Harris have to go AWOL for this mission."

CHAPTER FIFTEEN
KALEB

Fuck me. The look in her eyes is nothing short of a knife to the gut. She'll be giving up her life in more ways than one for this mission. Every damn thing she has fought to achieve and succeeded by doing so. This shit has been beating the hell out of my brain all damn morning.

After what we shared last night, the connection we now have, talking openly and freely for the past hour, I've ruined it.

The fire flares in her stare. A pissed-off Jade is sexy as fuck. Every time I fucked her before our last mission, I ended up treating her like shit, ordering her around, demanding she do exactly what I said.

Things are different here at home. I'm trying like hell to make this work, to let her in. When she asked about my brother, I became lost thinking about Kane. He has no place here. I don't want his name or his presence anywhere near her. He's tainted. And the worst bastard I've ever known.

This time is for us to get to know each other on a personal level, and this mission I'm about to discuss with her could fuck it all up. I'm not going to let it happen. No fucking way. If she's not willing to comply, then I won't try to convince her. She means too much to me. Whatever decision she makes, I will stand by her, but she needs to hear me out. She needs to understand why The President has asked this of us.

"Baby. Before you go all crazy on my ass, you need to let me explain. Remember these orders came from The President, this is not coming from me." She doesn't say a damn thing, only edges past me with her horse, her head down. She climbs off of him, ties his reins to a tree, and sits down several feet away from me. Fuck. She's distracting with her legs spread out in front of her, those boots on, and those fucking shorts that have my cock hard. I'm the biggest asshole to be thinking about fucking her up against a tree out here. Christ.

"Explain then. Tell me why I have to do this. Other than for the love of my country. Which I believe I've proven. This is our lives. It's all Harris and I know. We'll have nothing after this is over. The Army doesn't care why you go AWOL. We'll both be discharged. We'll lose everything. I'll have nothing. So you tell me why? Why would I want to do that, Kaleb?" I sit here watching her shake her head in exasperation. She looks defeated. Fuck, it kills me to the point I'm ready to say fuck it. I'll take someone else. But damn it, I can't. No matter what, she needs to understand.

I climb off the horse and pull him over to the same tree, securing him tightly. Then I go to her and kneel down directly in front of her, placing my hands on her thighs. Not sexually, but intimately.

"Like I said, these orders came from The President, Jade. He doesn't want ties to the Army or to him. This man is dangerous. He also has information he needs. Is this request uncommon? Yes. What I do know is, there is no way in hell he would ask someone to give up what they've fought their entire life to achieve if it weren't important for the safety of our country. Besides, do you really think he'd allow you to lose everything?" I sit back on my hunches and remove my hands from her silky skin. That same sullen expression on her face increases.

"If he doesn't want ties to the Army, then yes, Kaleb, I do lose everything. This is what those strange looks you and Harris were giving each other earlier are about, isn't it? He knows. You've asked him to do it too, haven't you? What did he say? Is he willing to give it all up?" Taking a deep, long breath, I tell her.

"He is. He doesn't like it any more than you do. Like I told him, the decision is yours. I'll support you either way. One thing I didn't tell him that I need for you to know is, whatever decision you make, it won't change the way I feel about you." Instantly, I dread her response. I watch her hackles rise. She recoils back in shock.

"I sure as hell would hope not." She draws her knees up to her chest.

"Christ, Jade. I apologize. Hell, maybe I need confirmation from you that it doesn't. Fuck, I don't know. We finally work this out and decide we're going to give this a shot, and then I drop this on you. You have to know you mean more to me than this mission. You and I have a long way to go to build something strong and beautiful. I want a lifetime. I'm fucking falling for you, Jade. Falling so hard for you that it scares the living shit out of me. I'm not going to lose you over this."

Her manner changes right before my eyes. I see it before she even has the chance to say it. She's falling for me too. This is a fucked-up situation we're in, starting with the way we met and my fucked-up infatuation to make her mine.

"I... I'm scared," she whispers.

"Scared of what? Me? Us? Your career?" I ask honestly.

"All of it."

"Jade. I'm not going to push you into making your decision. What I will push you on is us. You should know by now I'm a determined man. I don't give up on a damn thing. Not when I want something or someone. I want you so fucking bad I can't think straight at times. I want you in my bed every night. In my arms. I want to know what you want out of life. I want it all. And I want it with you." Never in my life would I have dreamed I would say that shit to a woman. This indescribable feeling of seeing a future with someone. Like I said, we have a long way to go, but there isn't a damn thing that will make me stop wanting or needing her. I don't give two fucks if I sound like a fucking pussy right now. I'm a man who wants this woman. It's plain and simple. One thing I do know is, when this mission is over, I'm not taking any more for a while. My first priority belongs to her.

Her features soften, and my fucking heart beats wildly in my chest as she stares out behind me. Her mind has to be racing. Christ, I can see the wheels spinning in her head from here.

When her gaze locks with mine, I clench my damn fist, fighting off the urge I have to pull her onto my lap and kiss the fuck out of her. That is until she speaks the words that nearly knock me backwards.

"I've already fallen for you, Kaleb. You've proven to me you'll catch me. Just don't drop me. I'm begging you not to. I'm going to need you when this is over." I jolt then. A man on a mission of his own, I grab her arms and haul her sexy little ass to me. This time I do fall. Flat on my back, pulling her down with me and her damn body flush on mine.

"As long as you run, I'll always catch you, Jade. I need some clarification here though, babe. Are you saying you'll do it? You can take some time, talk to Harris and see where his head is at before you make a decision that affects the rest of your life." Her expression softens even more. My mind flits back to how controlling this woman was when we first met. She was so stubborn, always challenging my every command and determined to take control. Her delicate side is peering her head. And fuck me, if that doesn't have my cock raging like a trapped lion in a damn cage ready to come out. I need to fuck her. Hard.

Her eyes sparkle from the intense sun. I see it in her eyes, the way she grinds her hips into mine, and the way her breathing turns ragged and those glistening eyes turn cloudy. To anyone else, this might be all kinds of fucked up, that we want to fuck out here in the open. She still hasn't answered my question. I'm not giving her what we both want until she does.

"You going to answer me? Or do I have to spank your ass to get it out of you?" I tease. Her lips pucker, and she twists them to the side of her gorgeous face. Thinking.

"If you need to spank me, then do it. But to answer your question. Yes, Sir. I'm willing to go on this mission. I wouldn't be able to live with myself if I didn't." I'd be a liar if I said I wasn't proud of her. She'll never have to worry about me not catching her, because the only time she's going to fall is when she falls all the way with me.

"I love it when you smile. And when you address me as Sir. You may want to remember that when I fuck you up against a tree. Now strip," I demand, watching the expressions on her face change.

"I'll strip, but the Sir part you can forget about." I quirk a brow. Then I lift a hand off of her firm ass and slap it hard. I swear to Christ the sound echoes. "Take everything off, Jade. Now."

"Tit for tat and all that, Maverick. You slap my ass again—" I cut her off by branding my mouth on hers. She needs to shut the hell up now. We have a hell of a lot to discuss still about this mission, but right now, I need to bury my cock in her.

I watch her stand after I kiss the hell out of her. Her plump lips are swollen, and my cock aches like a bitch to be inside her. Fuck, she slowly tugs her shirt over her head, exposing a damn pink lace bra doing nothing to hide the swell of her breast or her nipples begging for my mouth. She is the sexiest woman I have laid my eyes on, and she's mine. Every inch of her. She taunts me like the damn little seductress vixen she is when she shimmies those little shorts down her body, revealing her bare pussy to me. I can see how wet she is from here. If I didn't want to fuck her so damn bad, I would chew her ass out for not wearing any panties.

I curl myself up and stand, wasting no time and yanking my t-shirt over my head, then unsnapping and pulling the zipper down on my jeans with a speed of desperation. "As much as I want to swell those lips of yours more by having you on your hands and knees so I can fuck your mouth, my cock wants to feel your warmth. Wrap your hands around that tree directly behind you, Jade, and hold the fuck on." I bend and let my jeans fall to my knees all the while having my eyes trained to her ass.

I pick up my shirt. My cock is killing me when I walk over to her, tug her away from the tree, and place my shirt over her breast.

"I don't want the bark to scrape those beauties. I may have to fuck them later too." I push her forward, grab her hips, yanking her into the position I want her.

"God, Kaleb. I want you to fuck me," she moans, her words teetering on the edge of begging.

"Hang on, baby." I line my cock up to her sweetness and plunge inside of her. "Jesus Christ. You drive me out of my damn mind. It doesn't matter if I'm making love to you nice and slow or fucking your sweet pussy like a madman. Every time I slide my cock into you, I feel like I'm home." She gasps when I start pounding into her. My thrusts pick up pace if only to get inside of her as deeply as I can go.

My name is falling from her lips the whole time her pussy sucks me in with every deep drive. She grasps me tight with every outward stroke.

"Oh fuck!" she screams and I release one hand from her hip to grab a handful of her hair and pound her pussy like I own it. And I do, damn it. I lose control when I feel her hand right where we're connected. Circling her clit. Her pants becoming quicker, her ass shoving back against me, letting her warmth so close I swear she's damn near about to come all over my cock.

"Let go. Fucking milk me and come, Jade." I practically growl out in her ear, nibbling and sucking on her bottom lobe.

"Fuck," she whimpers out loudly, violently contracting her walls around my cock. I close my eyes and feel my release fill her. I may have said minutes ago I was falling. There's no doubt in my mind I've landed. I love her. Christ, I fucking love this woman, and I've got to be out of my fucking mind taking her on this mission.

JADE

Feeling him fuck me after such life-altering news doesn't cure the chaos in my mind. No, it only deters it until reality sets in again. I had no idea he was at a status to receive direct requests from The President himself. There's so much to this man I don't know, and I have mixed feelings about uncovering all that's hidden. I can tell he has a past that would make a great novel, but unfortunately, we don't have the time to cover everything from our pasts.

I'm extremely attracted to this man. He intrigues me sexually of course, but his intelligence has quickly become what I love most. I was beginning to think he didn't have what it took to be sensual with someone and he wouldn't be sensitive enough for me to fall for, but this man seems to have the perfect balance of all the above. He literally consumes me, and I find myself craving him when he's not near me.

This mission will be tough; going to a country that neither of us really know much about to pull out a terrorist without the support of the military I've grown to love. This will be interesting.

He tosses me his shirt to use to clean up the drips running down my legs. This leaves him shirtless and no doubt will raise questions from the other two, but I don't care. It's a simple gesture that I can appreciate and truly do.

"You okay?" His touch on my back as I bend to pull my shorts up startles me. He puts his arms around my naked back, and I let him hold me for a brief moment before the rest of our world erupts into the crazy planning of this mission.

"I'm good," I lie. I'm getting really good at that. Does he believe me though?

"After this mission, I want you to go away with me. We deserve peace and calm days with wild nights. I'll let you choose the place."

"I'd love that."

"You know I have to leave in the morning. I want nothing more than to stay with you, but I have to move."

"I know you do. I'm sure we'll leave in the morning too."

"I'll be working my ass off with my team, working on the logistics of the mission to make sure we're safe going in. We won't move if I have any doubt, Jade." I start to put the rest of my clothes on and just listen to him begin to strategize. The proof of his passion begins to show the more he talks.

"My guys will be irate that I'm bringing you in. They will accept you, but they'll be determined I'm thinking with my dick; but I'm standing by my decision to bring you. Jade, you are hands down the best sniper I've seen, and I'm proud as fuck to have you on this mission. You saved my ass in the last one, and I hope I never have to repay that favor, but if I have to, I'll lay down my life for you out there."

"Don't talk like that. Out there, we're a team. You can't focus on me any more than you do the guys. I won't have you treating me any differently. You know I hate that shit, Kaleb. I've earned my status, so treat me like I did not fuck my way onto this team." We both know I've earned every right to do this job and I do it well. Normally, I couldn't care less what others think of me, but these men are his friends. I don't know them like I do Harris and JJ, who know how hard I've worked to achieve my status. The real reason is because if things work out for us like I hope they do, I will be seeing a hell of a lot more of these guys. I need to earn their respect as well as their friendship. They're part of Kaleb's life and so am I.

"You didn't. I know that and if any of them want to go against you to prove you aren't the best, I'll let them try. My team is great, it really is. They're just not used to me bringing in new bodies and sure as fuck aren't used to me bringing in hot as fuck bodies." He slaps my ass as he finishes his statement.

"We're going to have to lay down some rules, Kaleb. Out there... you don't get to slap my ass. I don't want them knowing that we're fucking. I'll tell Harris to keep that shit private and he will. We're going back to you being my Commander, but this time without the nighttime meetups. I want all focus on the mission and keeping the team safe."

"I agree. I won't tell them anything, but it will kill me when they start to talk about you and I can't rip their dicks off. Because I know the second they see you, they'll talk about fucking your sweet ass. They're men. They aren't dead." I almost laugh. Almost. A jealous Kaleb is a sexy Kaleb. He needs to know though, whatever we have stays here.

"Just bite your tongue and let it roll off of you. You and I know who will be hitting this when we get back home." I slap my ass playfully, smiling at him as I walk away from him before he can copy me.

"I sure as fuck will, but first I'm keeping you up all night long." We start to walk back to the horses. Who would've ever thought we'd be out here like this right now, talking about the single most dangerous mission, and the one thing we're worried about is what the others think. I've seen it too many times. If the team thinks there's favoritism, it won't work as well, and this isn't the time to test the emotions of an entire group of men I've never met.

"We should get back to the house and see what Harris wants to do tonight."

"You know he's fucking Mallory."

"Kaleb. He is not."

"Let's bet on that." His eyes travel to my ass. Jerk. I'd give myself over to him just for the pleasure he brings me. I'm not betting him that he can take my ass over something I hope like hell is happening or will happen. He may be right, but I ignore him. Harris and Mal deserve to have some fun, and I know neither of them is insane, so I don't have anything against them finding time together. I step over the saddle and lean forward to watch Kaleb get on his horse as well. We head back at a much slower pace than before and enjoy the view the whole way. He shares more of his life with me, and I absorb every word he says.

CHAPTER SIXTEEN
JADE

I'm watching Harris on the grill and Kaleb standing to his right with a beer in his hand. I know they're talking mission, and I'm okay with that. They're bonding, and that's important to me. I'm actually surprised Kaleb chose to bring Harris on the mission, considering their history, but it makes me feel better knowing he can put aside his issues and acknowledge talent when he sees it.

Mallory is talking, and I'm doing my best to spend as much time with her before I have to leave again.

"Do you know when you'll be leaving again?"

"Soon."

"Damn it. I was hoping that I'd get you for a few months before you went again."

"I'm hoping it'll be short this time." My eyes drift back to the guys, and I watch them both smile.

"You know I'll be here, and be sure you bring his sexy ass back with you." She nods her head in Harris' direction, and I can't help but interrogate her ass.

"How was the horse ride?"

"It was so peaceful, Jade. I'm definitely going to have to ride again."

"Are we talking a horse or Harris?"

"Both would be nice, but I'm talking about the horse, you crazy ass."

"Well, I couldn't tell by the way you look at him."

"Ehh. He's hot, but so many of them are."

"Harris is a great guy. He's a riot to be around."

"Yeah, I've noticed. I've laughed more today than I have in I don't know how long."

"That's great, Mal."

"I'm guessing you weren't laughing so much on your ride."
She softly punches my arm, and I laugh at her sorry attempt of
hiding that something happened while they were out there.

"No really, we didn't do anything. We just talked about life
and shit. He's an interesting guy, and I just loved getting his
opinion on things."

"Maybe we'll be able to try this trip again when we return." I
say. I'm not one to pry. Well, I am, but not here in front of
everyone. She'll spill her guts out when we get back from this
mission.

"I'd love that!" We spend the rest of the evening doing things
normal people do every day, and I enjoy every minute of it. It's
the simple things like curling my legs up under me on the couch
and drinking a cup of coffee or cooking dinner in a fully
equipped kitchen, even though the meat was cooked outside on
the grill. We keep talking about politics and vacation
destinations until we're all dying to go somewhere tropical with
beaches and water surrounding us.

"I'd love to go somewhere like Mexico to eat their authentic
food and experience their culture." Mallory freezes us all when
she starts to speak. We all play it off decently well when the
initial surprise wears off.

"Nah. Mexico would be fun, but I'm thinking maybe an
island somewhere. I'd love the privacy." Harris insinuates so
much with his statement, not to mention his eyes, when he says
privacy. Kaleb jerks his head in my direction. His brows lift in a
challenging way, and I roll my eyes at him. I won't admit to him
his suspicions are spot-on. No way.

"Well, I think I'm going to bed. I have to head out early, and
I'm going to be selfish and take Jade to bed. You two don't mind
us if you hear screaming."

"Kaleb. What the hell?" They all start to laugh, and I stand as
he takes me by the hand and pulls me up.

"Yes, old Maverick is a screamer." I swat his ass with my free hand.

"I'll show your ass a screamer." He continues to hold my hand as he twirls me once then wraps his arms around me, talking to them with his chin over my shoulder.

"Okay. Good night, you two. Mallory and I will have to play a drinking game or something out here to try to drown out your noise if you're going to go like that." Harris is smiling, while Mallory looks slightly nervous. She can handle herself, and I know they'll enjoy whatever they actually do. *Like fuck again.*

"Night." Before I get to say much, Kaleb is walking forward, causing me to do the same with him right behind me. His playful hands as we continue down the hall introduce me to this softer side of him. A side of him that's simple and carefree. A side I could really get used to.

Once the door closes behind us, he turns me to face him, and we just breathe each other in. Our foreheads resting on each other and the tips of our noses touching. "I'm never going to want tonight to end." My words escape before I realize I'm thinking out loud.

He takes both of my hands and pulls them to his mouth. I welcome his soft invasion. He twines our hand together, blanketing them in between our bodies. His slow, maneuvering tongue sweeps across my bottom lip, beginning to unwind me and my beating heart as I feel the intensity rise inside my body. This man has approached me in different styles when it comes to sex, and I can't even tell you which I prefer, because I love what he does to me every time we're together. He keeps me on my toes, and I find it intriguing that I honestly have no idea what he'll do next. I'm waiting for his aggressive side to kick in, but it doesn't.

He removes my clothes slowly and sensually, walking around me, taking me in after he exposes me fully. He pulls his own shirt off and stands in front of me like he wants to say something, but he never does. He moves in to kiss me, and I kiss him back with the urgency he has caused. I want him now and I want him fast, but he has different plans.

His kiss softens slightly as he slows us down, and we literally kiss for what has to be a half hour. Tongues twirling, slowly and passionately, while our hands explore each other's bodies. His caresses are soft and sensual across my skin. We don't take it to the next level until he lays me on the bed and begins to kiss my body. The air leaves me as he leaves a trail of moisture from his tongue down my neck, around my breasts, and down my stomach until he's between my legs, making me squirm. One long, delicate stroke across my center and my back bows off the bed, causing me to moan and leaving me wanting more.

"You taste so fucking good, Jade. Your bare little pussy is so perfect, and I can't believe how much I want you right now." He moves down further between my legs, kissing my thighs as he continues to talk.

"You're ruining me, Jade. You're destroying me in ways I never thought possible, and I love every fucking second of it." He moves over me until he's straddling my waist, pinning me down with his weight. I watch him lower his head to mine and feel him as he moves my wrists together into one of his hands.

"I can't fucking wait to do so many things to you. Our sex life will never be boring." His mouth continues to move over my neck and chest as he slides his body down mine before he settles between my legs and enters me so slowly. I fight the urge to thrust my own hips to hurry him along, but I don't give in. I wait for him with so much anticipation I want to scream.

"I'll tie you up and pound..." He thrusts hard once as he continues, "this sweet pussy every single fucking day if you let me." His eyes lock into mine, and I listen to his promises, knowing some would consider them threats. He doesn't scare me, he turns me the fuck on, and I practically orgasm to his words.

"And that ass. Your tight, perfect little ass. Fuck, Jade. You were made for me." He moves slowly in and out of me, building my desire with every touch from him, including his words.

"I'll blindfold you. I'd love to watch you finger yourself when you have no idea where I'm at or what I'm doing." He continues to move through me.

"I'll fuck you against everything you can imagine. It'll just be you and I, Jade. My dick in your pussy every time you want it."

My sex drive is screaming 'fuckkkk yes!' to his promises. I can't take another word as I manage to roll my hips forward and he hits me just perfectly, sending me into an explosive orgasm, sounds of pleasure pouring out of me. There's no doubt I can be heard, but I really don't care as he begins to move harder and faster.

"That's it, Jade, let me hear you. You're so fucking sexy." He fucks me and I let him. His grip is still holding my arms above my head in one hand, positioning his face so close to mine. Our eyes are locked onto each other's while our breaths hit each other with every thrust forward.

"Fuck. You feel so good on my cock."

Yes, I do feel great when I'm on his cock. He makes me feel like no other man has. I can tell he truly cherishes me, and it feels amazing to have someone desire me like he does. He thinks I'm ruining him.... I think he's already ruined me. I'll never be able to be with another man without comparing him to this right here. Can he make me feel like I do right in this very second? I've found my fullness, and I don't want to ever lose it.

He moves us to the edge of the bed, allowing my wrists free and my head slightly hanging off the edge. The blood rushes to my head, intensifying everything, and I begin a very loud release yet again. His final thrusts are the best because of the warmth he fills me with every time he slams against me.

"I love how you sound when I fuck you." Oh god, I love it too, but I can't talk right now. The feeling of complete satisfaction has made me a lifeless mess of exhaustion, and I let him wrap me up in his arms and hold me while I quickly fall asleep.

KALEB

Leaving her is one of the hardest things I've ever done. Its right there, dead-even with when I left for basic training all those years ago, watching my mom and sister balling.

Jade had tears in her eyes when I held her in my arms this morning. It made me smile into the mess of her hair when she said she was crying because she wanted to spend more time with me. Not because the next time we see each other, we'll be in full combat mode. I loved hearing her say that. I love even more that when this is over, we'll take off somewhere. Sure as shit won't be Mexico. No fucking way. It will be tropical. Where I can watch her parade around in a bikini. Fuck. Maybe not. Maybe it should be the Swiss Alps, where she's covered up in ski gear. That way I won't be beating every man's ass who looks her way.

"You're an idiot, Maverick. That woman only wants you. Dominate in the bedroom only, you asshole. She's the one who's dominated your ass." I laugh. Now I'm talking to myself.

I turn on the stereo, flipping through every channel I can find. "Jesus, I like country, but fuck. Not a single damn classic rock station." I settle on some shit I've never heard of and put my mind to this mission. To capture this asshole and get the hell out of there. Before I know it, I'm pulling into the gates of the compound.

It's been a while since I've been here. Our home away from home. Our safe place. Log cabins nestled in the woods. Ten acres between us separating each other, yet close enough that if anyone found out about us being here, we wouldn't have far to get to each other.

I pull my truck up to the office after shutting the gate up tight with the remote and park it alongside Pierce's truck.

"It's about damn time, fuckface. Kase said you had business in Alabama. You care to share?" That damn devious expression of his needs to be slapped off his face.

"No. It's my business, not yours, dickhead. What the hell are you doing here anyway? Don't tell me you're our personal contact to The President?" Pierce snaps his head back as if I'd bitch slapped him.

"Well, fuck you too."

"Shit. You are. Damn man, are you sure you can handle a gun? I mean, you've been behind a desk for how long now?" I'm goading him, and he hates that shit. He's always so touchy about his desk job. While Harris can speak any language under the damn sun, Pierce was born and raised in South Texas. He knows Spanish as well as English, and he has one of the best aims with a knife out of anyone I have ever seen.

"When you have no idea what the hell people are saying, you'll be glad I have your back. Now go help Kase with the beer and chips. Seems the fucker lost his way." Our threesome has always been this way. Easy bullshit. Tease a little. We're real. A bond only to be shared between the three of us. It's authentic to a point no one will ever get in, nor will they understand the things we've been through. I served months overseas with these two and battled and killed alongside both of them. We've saved each other's lives and talked into the dead of night about our families and home. We would die for each other, and we've always promised that none of us would be left behind.

"He's hiding here. It's an old, abandoned building in the middle of Tonala, Mexico. It's busy as hell down there. This place is known for all of its markets and vendors. He's smart. I give him credit." Pierce takes a sip of his beer while showing us the map. The town is down by Guadalajara. Busy as hell is right. Street vendors selling their hard work everywhere. It'll be full of innocent people.

These fucking men we go after don't give two shits if the men and women who work their asses off are killed or not, but we sure as hell do.

"It looks like another night raid. It still won't be easy. Some of these places are open all night. There're tons of bars. And foreigners will be on vacation. We're going to have to walk in and escort that bastard out," I tell them both frustratingly.

"Not necessarily. Look behind this building. It's an open field for at least a half mile. I think we're definitely in for a night drop, but it's nothing we haven't done before. We got this shit." I quirk my brow at Kase, while we watch Pierce tap away in confidence on the computer bringing up different angles. He moves his mouse here and there, marking with an X. This is his expertise. It's the reason they wanted him working for the government. He can work you into the smallest hole and help you weasel your way out.

"Done. Now." He spins around in his chair. "Tell us about these two specialist. It's obvious they impressed you." That's an understatement if I've ever heard one.

"Captain Harris and Captain Elliott of the United States Army Special Forces. Harris is a translator and one hell of a shooter. He's confident in everything he does." I pause briefly. Christ, I know these guys, they love women as much as I do, but neither one of them has battled alongside one before. My temper flares before I even tell them about her. I slam it back down my throat before they catch wind to the fact there's more to me and Jade than what I'm about to tell them.

"And Elliott?" Kase presses.

"Captain Jade Elliott," I announce.

"What? A woman? Explain, asshole." Pierce slams his beer down on the desk.

"I've heard of her. She's the first woman to make it through Ranger school. Well, there were several of them, but fuck, I had no idea she was on this last mission with you." There are a lot of things about her they don't know, and I need to keep it that way. My hands want to clench in a fist and punch him in his damn mouth for his reaction.

"She's damn good. Not only did she save my life out there by killing a young boy we never saw, but she can shoot like no one else I've ever seen, and I mean ever. She's good, really fucking good, and I want her." They both look at me like I've lost my mind or I'm growing another head and it doesn't resemble the one currently sitting on my shoulders.

"What the hell do you mean you want her? Have you been fucking her?" My anger spreads from Pierce to Kase when he talks to me like he's my parent.

"Hell, no. What the hell is your problem? She's a woman. And a soldier. A damn fine one. She's willing to give up her career for this, just like Harris. The only difference between the two of them is, she has a pussy and he has a dick. But that woman has balls like a damn man when it comes to her job. She's dedicated." I need to shut the fuck up about her. The three of us are partners, yes, but each one of us has a specialty in how we run our business, and they damn well know mine is setting up the best team I can find.

"You like her," Pierce says more out of curiosity than a question.

"Of course I do. She's a damn good soldier." He smirks at my answer.

"That's not what I mean and you know it, Maverick. You like this woman. She means something to you. I can see it all over your damn face. There's no denying it. Shit, man. I hope to god you know what the fuck you're doing." I stand there for the longest damn time, my gaze darting back and forth between my two best friends. My brothers.

"Listen. I'm not going into details with the two of you about what's happening between Jade and I, but come the fuck on. Do you really think I would jeopardize anyone's life? This woman knows what the hell she's doing, and for the two of you to say otherwise is nothing but pure bullshit." I sink my ass down in the chair and let them think about their reaction to what they are actually saying. It's wrong.

"We know you wouldn't put anyone's life on the line. That's not what the problem is here. The problem is you. I'm concerned for you. Can you handle being out there with her? Watching her back while still leading this team?" Kase asks. Then he slugs down the rest of his beer.

"I get it. And I'm damn happy for you, man. I truly am. I hope she's the one; hell, I would gladly welcome her into our family if she is. We just need to know that your head is clear and that you shoved aside the fact you care about her. If you can look at us and tell us you can, then great. This conversation is over. Done. But if you lie to us like you did when you said you weren't fucking her, then man, we have a serious fucking problem here. These orders come from The President. You need to keep your shit under control. Let her do her job and get all of us the hell out of there." Kase rubs his hand across his forehead in complete testiness.

"I can handle it. She was with me once before, remember? That's where it all started. I completed my mission, successfully I might add. Trust me, I know what I'm doing. The choice is yours to believe me or not. And I get where you're coming from. Who knows, if the tables were turned, I might feel the same way. I'm asking you this though. And listen to me, okay? She doesn't want you two to know. In fact, I gave her my word I wouldn't tell you." Kase's lips twitch. Pierce doesn't hesitate to lean his head back and fucking laugh. The bastard. This shit means something to her and he's laughing.

"What the fuck, asshole?" I lean forward and punch him in the gut. This is serious shit.

"You, man. Your head's tripping over this chick. I fucking love it. Now I really can't wait to meet her. Hell, I'm counting the days down now." And fuck me. Just like that, the three of us sit around, finish up our business, and call it a night. The last thing I say as I walk out the door is, "Keep your eyes off of her. If you even look at her ass, I swear to fucking god I will shove a stick of dynamite up yours and light that bitch."

CHAPTER SEVENTEEN
JADE

Kaleb reached out to both Harris and I, saying he needs us to fly to the compound. He's sending a private plane, and we're supposed to be there tonight to meet the entire team and organize the Intel they've received on our guy. My nerves are a little shot about this mission, but I'm sure it's just that I'm going in with only Harris and Maverick at my back as of right now. I'm hoping I'll feel better once I meet them all.

My emotions are mixed with the nerves of the mission and with meeting Kaleb's two best friends.

"I wish you weren't leaving. Can you please promise you'll call me as soon as you can? I can tell you guys are all up to something big, and I'll respect you enough to not ask any questions." Mallory throws her arms around my shoulders before she pulls me in tight for a nice hug.

"I'll call when I can." I hold her just as tight.

"I know you will eventually, but shit, I'm worried, so please make it soon." I need to go. My head needs to be in the game, so I pull away from her. I can't be touched right now, not even in a caring way. It's time to get my head on straight for this mission.

"Be ready for that pamper day you keep asking me about. I'm due for one soon, and it would be a great thing to look forward to when I get back," I say truthfully.

"For sure. Now please be careful, and if you get a chance to talk good about me to Beau, I'd really appreciate it."

"You know I will, but you have to tell me how it all went at the ranch." My phone begins to vibrate mid-sentence. It's Harris. Shit, that was fast.

"Elliott, I'm pulling onto your street now, we have to leave, so meet me outside." He seems stressed and bossy as hell, but I begin to grab my single bag of belongings, knowing I won't have much room for anything on this mission.

"Mal, I have to go now. I love you, girl, and I'll be in touch as soon as I can."

"Love you too. Be safe." I turn and walk out the door as I let the rush of the situation wash over me. I didn't dare tell her how dangerous this mission is. I could never deal with the look on her face if she realized the severity of this. My mom and dad kept telling me to be safe too when I called them to cancel. Of course I'll be safe. There's no other option.

"You ready to do this?" Harris is walking up the driveway when I step outside.

"You bet your ass." Confidence and clarity are vital. I'll be using this flight to get my clarity in check. My confidence comes easy.

We both start talking about what we know about the mission, which isn't much. The drive to the private plane is very short, and there's an oversized hanger we're instructed to pull his truck inside of. I grab my bag and take a deep breath. Harris just moves without a thought, so I draw from his courage at the moment and step out of the truck to start this journey.

"Morning. Captain Harris and Captain Elliott, I'll be your pilot." I watch a massive silhouette walk into the hanger out of the bright sunshine. His swagger is cocky and confident, and I'm instantly intrigued.

"Name is Trevor. We don't have time for you to gawk at me, ma'am. We have to move." Harris smiles as we both walk, directly following this Trevor guy. My eyes do fall on his perfect ass for a short second before I catch myself. Shit, I'm going to have to watch that.

The flight takes a few hours, and Harris and I don't talk much. He talks to the pilot as we fly across part of the US, and I find my peace and clarity.

This is my life now. Exactly what I'm trained to do and the very thing I prayed I'd have the opportunity to be a part of. A mission like this only comes to an elite group, and I'm now going on two back to back. Going AWOL was an easy decision once I found out who we're going in for. My superior didn't give me any issues when I reported my status. I didn't share any details about this mission with him, which he didn't ask about either. He seemed more concerned about me having clearance from the psych evaluations.

My mind shifts to Kaleb. Honestly, I'm excited to see this side of him. Not many men can lead something like this using only private resources. His dedication to his career is evident in the way this is all playing out, and I can't tell you how sexy that is to me. A man who knows what he wants and goes after it is a man who gets things done. He's determined, and I can only hope he continues to be focused on me once we all return from this mission.

We land before I know it, and this is when everything goes quickly. We follow Trevor into a Hummer that's waiting for us, drive a few minutes across a field, then pull up next to a log house that appears to be very new. I'm working overtime to pull in all I can as I look around to know my surroundings. Three more log cabin style homes in view and a dog on my left. Two men standing next to a helicopter and another three in front of the house we pull up to. Movement toward us pulls my focus back to the men by the helicopter.

Once we're all standing near, Kaleb steps out of the house, and I feel my tension decrease. My anxiety falls slightly, and I don't miss his stare straight into my heart. The hungry look in his eyes matches mine, and I decide right then that he matches my cravings when it comes to the adrenaline of this kind of stuff.

"Captain Elliott, Captain Harris, this is my team. You've met the pilot Steele, this is Bullet, Tank, Ace, and Vice, and that grinning fool over there is Action Jackson. Everyone come inside, so I can brief you before we leave out."

He stands holding the front door open, allowing everyone through as he watches me. I wait till the end to walk up and feel the warmth of his smile move over me in this otherwise cold situation. Tension is definitely in the air when I step through the door and look at the men standing together in the large living area. A few begin to sit at the long dining room table, so the rest of us follow.

"We don't have much time. Pierce, get the images up." He brushes his hand across my back as he passes me to take his spot at the head of the table, allowing him access to the technology surrounding us. The guy he called Ace earlier begins to put information on the large wall behind Kaleb's back.

"This is Al-Quaren. He has a few look-a-likes surrounding him at all times, so we're looking for these specific markings." He shows scars on the target's arm and neck as well as a small mole on the side of his face. His features are hard to see with the thaub he seems to always wear. "I need him alive. We go in and pick him up. If you're in this room, I expect you to have anyone else's back in here as if you'd have mine. This is a big mission for me before I take some much needed fucking time off. These orders came from The President himself, so don't fuck this up."

"We're flying in tonight then immediately boarding a waiting truck . We'll reach the drop locations later that night. We'll go in, fuck shit up, grab his ass, and then get the fuck out. Here are the pictures of his pussy sidekicks you have my permission to blow their heads off once you verify it's not our guy." He begins to show us pictures of five men who look very similar. I work to notice noses, lips, and eyes, focusing on the slightest differences.

"Each of you will have a packet with all of this information. I want you studying the shit out of it on the flight. Know these fuckers like you'd know your own mom before we land that bird."

I stop obsessing just slightly, knowing I'll have another chance to look. Kaleb keeps his focus on the mission and does very well hiding our relationship from the guys, which I'm thankful for.

"You each have a bag with your gear in it and your fake IDs with clearance back into the US in the event there are any problems. I've given you everything we need to do this without limitations. You'll have heat and night vision capabilities, and your weapons are the ones you're used to using. There's no time to be hesitating even one single fucking second out here. Wear your goddamn vests and headgear with the rest of the clothes and this should go easy." He pauses to look at me for just a slight second.

"Have each other's backs. This is a ride or die team, and I want you to include Harris and Elliott in on that. I promise you they have the talent to save your asses out here." His intense stare into his team's eyes leaves no room for discussion. This is him protecting me. I know this. He knows this.

"If there aren't any questions, let's load the fuck up and do this. Wear your civilian clothes until we reach Mexico. We'll have a place to change when we reach the gear that's already been delivered." The guys all move to their feet quickly, and I follow just shortly after. I'm moving through the door and past Kaleb when he pulls me back against his chest, closing the door.

"Why are you so fucking distracting? I love watching your eyes when you listen to me talk. You're so damn beautiful it makes my dick hard knowing I'll be taking you away on that trip I promised." He slides his palm down my arms, and I feel him everywhere. "Have you picked the place?"

"Not yet." I turn to face him, allowing my hands to touch his chest.

"Well, you need to figure it out, because we leave in about four fucking days." He leans down to kiss me, and I allow him for a few seconds, kissing him back before we have to make an appearance outside. This time in here goes against everything we planned, and I'm not risking the bullshit if they find out.

"I told Kase and Pierce about us."

"Kaleb, what the fuck?"

"I had to. They'd have guessed in one fucking second anyway. I wanted them to hear from my mouth I have my head on straight, so they don't start doubting me out there. I'm clear as fuck and they needed to see that."

"Okay, but they'd better not give me any shit."

"They won't. Now get out there before I have to tell the rest of those fuckers." He slaps my ass and opens the door. I give him the eye before I walk out, clearly swaying my ass on purpose until I'm in view of the rest of the team. Let him sit on that.

I take the packet Trevor hands me, then move to the empty seat at the back and immediately start studying. Every single bit of information could make a difference out there. I'm so focused that I miss Kaleb boarding, and before I know it, we're moving.

I listen to the guys give each other hell and watch Harris join right in. He fits well with these guys; hell, he fits with any team. He's one of those people who could work any room in record time. I'm more the quiet, reserved type when it comes to a group like this. I observe then prove myself with my actions. I've learned that's the only way to shut anyone up anyway.

"Hey Elliott, you too good to cut the shit with us?" Jackson turns to call me out on being impersonal.

"I'm not here to talk to you guys, I'm here to successfully get through this mission. If you want to talk to me, look me up after." Kaleb's eyes go wide, and I wait for his smartass mouth, but he holds back whatever he was about to say.

"Damn, didn't peg you for a bitch." Jackson's words might've cut deep if I hadn't heard them my whole career. Kaleb doesn't have to say a word this time, because Harris does it for him.

"Shut your fucking mouth. She'll be the one watching your ass out there. You want her hardened and ready for this fucking mission. Stay the fuck out of her head and let her do her thing."

Jackson looks at me once more, then sits back. I can see his wheels turning, and I have no idea what he's thinking. I'm sure he'll make it clear eventually.

Bullet unbuckles his belt and moves through the tiny space to sit near me. Kaleb turns to face forward, and I return to looking at terrorist information.

"Don't pay any attention to Jackson. He's our social butterfly. He likes to run his mouth, but he's a fucking beast in the field." I nod slightly, giving him the clarification he's after. I'm good.

"I'm used to the stereotype. It's all good."

"My name is Kase. I go by Bullet on this team."

"Nice caller. Do I need to pick mine?" I say, hoping he lets me.

"No, they'll give you one soon if they haven't already." Oh, great. I can just hear it. Bitch or cunt. Or something along those lines.

"Great, I can't wait."

"Don't you worry. If you don't like it, Maverick will lay them out. I can already see my boy is whipped." Well, shit. That didn't work or last long. I'm curious what all was said now though.

"You can?" He nods with a huge smile, showing off the most perfect teeth I've ever seen.

"Oh yeah. I've known him for more years than I'd like to share, and I've never seen him talk about a woman like he did about you."

"Please don't tell the others until this is over. I don't want people thinking I fucked my way onto this mission or any others I may get on."

"I gave my word to Maverick. You don't need a promise from me. Besides, Jade, your work, stamina, and courage speak for itself. It's not every day a woman achieves what you have. I'm damn proud to have you on this team. I can't wait to see more women in active duty. In my opinion, they deserve it and they've earned it." I like this guy. He's honest and not afraid to stand outside the normal realm of thinking.

"Thank you." I see Kaleb turn around to talk to Harris and watch the features on his face. He's relaxed. He's in his element and ready to thrive. I burn this view into my memory before I go back to studying the enemy.

That landing was smooth, and we stay inside until the plane rolls into another hanger. The door opens, and the hot air fills the cabin instantly.

"Welcome to Mexico, my friends." An old man and woman greet us in the building. "But you've got to hurry." We rush to grab our gear, while he points to an old farm truck with wood as sides for the bed of the truck. We're surrounded by the stench of shit, but it's nothing new to us.

The old man moves to the driver's seat, and we're moving again before we have a chance to think. "We have twenty miles until we reach the chopper. We have time there to regroup." Kaleb makes sure he's sitting near me this time, and I watch out the side of the truck, looking for any signs of activity around us.

"They're naming you Ice. We'll use that name throughout the mission. I felt it was fitting enough." I honestly kind of like it, it's a name I can deal with. I'm surprised they don't have Queen behind it though. Ice works either way.

"They tried to name Harris Pretty Boy, but I vetoed that. He'll be Stone." We don't use names on missions. It's call names only.

"Got it."

"I go by Fire on missions." I can't hold back my laughter.

"Of course you do."

"I thought you'd like that."

"Oh, it's very fitting." Fire and Ice. I'm dying inside. It's fucking perfect.

"Fire, you need to kill that fuckin smile. It's time to be focused on getting that motherfucker." Bullet leans in to reel

Kaleb in. I hold my smile in. I can't wait to chill with these guys outside of a stressful mission.

The rough ride to the chopper finally ends, and we all pile out and move inside an old house. We're greeted by a Caucasian man who seems even older than the man who drove us here.

"Okay, everyone, get your asses in your gear and be ready to move in ten. I want to show you the layout of the house he's hiding in. The truck will drop us close, then the chopper is how we'll get the fuck out." The guys begin taking off their shirts and I follow. This sports bra hides everything I need to hide, but shit if my eyes are working hard to betray me. These guys are all ripped. I could tell they were built, but had no idea how cut they were. This is a different caliber of man than I'm used to being surrounded by in the Army. Harris fits in here more than he ever did with the guys we were around in the Army.

Then they begin to stand in their underwear. Kaleb watches me as I have no issues standing in my panties and bra putting on the gear meant to fit tight and give me an edge up on the enemy. All black, thick enough to keep me from getting hurt as I crawl through whatever shit I'll have to, and fire resistant to top it off. The headgear is the exact same as what we used on our last mission. This transition is easy, but I know he made it that way.

Pulling my boots on, I catch his eyes again and give him a smile, knowing the little stunt I just pulled will have my ass in trouble later, but that's a price I'm willing to pay to watch him squirm a bit. It's a game I'm learning to love.

"Alright, let's go."

"Fire, I'll lead us off here." Jackson leans in, and the guys all surround him, so Harris and I follow. "May this day go well, so I can soon feel the swell of my dick going into some pussy. Because I'm not afraid to lick my way to the top and get me some nice, tight titties. Give me some ass that'll have me begging, and let this day go in the history books as bangin'. It's time to get this motherfucker, so I can keep my reputation, because I've got some

MILFs just waitin'." The little laughter coming from the group brings a smile to my face as all eyes move to me.

"May this day go well, so I can soon feel a dick filling my sweet pussy. Because I'm not afraid to lick my way to the tip and get me some nice-tasting liquid. I've got the ass that'll have him beggin', so let this day go down in the history books as bangin'.... As Mr. Action says." I clear my throat and pause as I feel the glare from Kaleb igniting me. "It's time to get this motherfucker, so I can keep my reputation as the Sniper they're all hating." The guys erupt in hysterical laughter, and I know this won't be the end of the back and forth banter between this group and I. I'm made for this shit. Having so many brothers prepared me for a day like today. I need them to see I'm not all ice. There's a little fire inside there too.

"Alright, alright. We can do this shit back at the compound when we celebrate this mission. Until then... Not another word about pussy and dick or licking any fucking thing. I want all focus on this damn mission and getting me home for the time off I need. I think I'm going to need more after that fucking speech." I know I'm getting to him and that's okay, because he's already fucking got to me. I get near him and feel his intensity. It doesn't hurt for him to feel the same.

"Here's the house. We're going in at this point, then Ice and Bullet will head to the top of this building. It's late out and that's far enough away from the house that you should be clear of their bullshit security spotting you. Bullet knows the entryway, so Ice, just stick close to him. The rest of us will split up and go here... and here." He points to the opposite sides of the house. From the looks of the map, this house is on the edge of a small village. Thoughts go through my head instantly about the very huge possibility that I'll run into the same nightmare as I did the last mission. Taking a deep breath, I prepare myself for just that. I have to do what it takes to make sure we all get out of there alive and fully intact.

"We get him alive and take him home. Steele will be listening in the chopper and will drop down for all of us right here. Once you hear the clear, get your asses to that chopper that will drop between the house and where Ice and Bullet are watching us." Everyone shifts just slightly as he stands to place his knives and guns in their places on his body. We all follow his lead, and I get a feel of the rifle he hands me.

"It's go time. Get back in the truck and let the old man get us to our locations. He knows this area and will be vital to us moving around tonight." Three o'clock in the morning and we're off. All the guys follow his orders, and I follow behind, knowing he'll have something to say to me before we leave.

"Please be smart out there. I want you safe."

"Kaleb. You know I'm great at what I do. I'll be fine. Don't baby me, damn it."

"I'm not. I just can't wait to fucking go away somewhere with you and have all of this shit behind us."

"What did you say, four days and we're leaving? You can wait that long." I choke back a laugh.

"I sure as fuck hope I can wait that long to feel you around my dick. Quit your damn testing me or I'll make you regret that shit when we get back."

"Oh, I sure hope you do." His eyes widen, and he's visibly struggling. I know if we had even five minutes, he'd pull me to the side and fuck me good. I wish we had ten minutes, but we don't. After this mission, we'll have a few weeks together and can make up for it then.

"You be safe, Kaleb. I'll be watching your ass for you."

"I know you will." We both look into each other's eyes without any further words. Our eyes are screaming to say more, but the time doesn't allow it. I turn to walk away and feel the depth of his stare as I do. This team has to feel the chemistry from us. I don't know what the hell I was thinking when I thought we could hide this.

Tank hits the top of the truck twice, and the old man starts to move us. "He won't be stopping, just slowing down, so be ready to drop and roll when it's time." Tank starts to instruct all of us on the drop. When it's time, we get the signal, and I go. The rifles are tossed out in their protective bags right behind us, and we quickly throw them over our shoulders and move to get out of sight. Trying to keep my heart calm, I try to zero in on Kaleb and the reason I want to get this over with soon.

"Here." Bullet is moving quickly, and I stay on his heels until we're moving on the roof of a building. It's rectangular-shaped, and one end faces the direction we need to be watching. We set up near each other in the center of the wall and start looking for our team. The first drop is made, and I listen to them talk in my ear as we wait for the second. My heart is pounding. I'm sweating. I want this done.

They're all moving in on the target quickly, and I look for any sign of anything I would need to shoot. So far, it's very quiet and I hate it. Why is it so fucking quiet? The guys are breathing, I can hear them in my ears, so I know they're all good, but I just have an eerie feeling. I stand to look behind us and see no signs of life. Trying to feel more relaxed, I face forward again and watch through my scope.

I finally see movement from one of our guys and signal to Bullet that I'm watching the front. He takes the back. Our guys move in, and I watch them take out a man with a knife. Kaleb and Harris are both in my sight, and I watch the surrounding area, waiting for so much as a fucking plant to move. They make their way inside, and we lose visibility of our team as all fucking hell blows up in that house.

The sounds of gunshots and screaming have me desperately listening for the voices I want to hear most. "Where is Al-Quaren?" Kaleb begins yelling, and Harris starts to speak in foreign, trying to get them to talk. I keep hearing gunshots and then notice movement in the front. Our team is all inside, so I know it's not one of ours.

Bullet sends off a shot and starts talking quietly. "You have them coming in. We're shooting out here." I send off two shots, taking out two in my view, quickly seeing three more ambushing the house quickly. I work fast to take them all out, hearing just as many shots coming from Bullet.

"Get the fuck out of there. There's a fuck ton coming your way. NOW, Fire. Get the fuck out now." I start shooting as fast as I'm trained to do, not missing a single shot, but knowing at least one got past me. I have eleven shots before I have to reload.

"There are too many of these fuckers. Get the fuck out. Get the chopper here, now. We have to move." Bullet starts giving orders, and I'm not sure if that makes it official or not.

"I have his ass, Fire. He's under the floor. I want to blow his fucking head off more than anything, but I'm holding him. I need someone back here, he's got four kids with him." Jackson's voice is desperate and loud in my ears.

"You sure it's him?" Kaleb questions.

"Yes, all three markings are here. Get back here and help me pull him out of this hole."

"Stone, get the fuck back there and tell him to move or we'll blow his ass up." I hear Kaleb giving orders and more shots going off. I get a small break in movement, so I reload, preparing for whatever is sent my way. Bullet shoots once more, and we both begin our scan of the area again.

"Come on, motherfucker. Crawl out of there." Listening to the sounds of the team fight their way to get him out makes my adrenaline rush even harder. I can hear them all struggle, and I wish we were in there to help.

"Okay. Fuck, we've got him out. Get the chopper here now." Kaleb sounds frustrated, and I can hear the loud sounds of the rest of the guys making their way out of the house. Bullet and I watch until the sounds of the chopper are near. The team has moved outside, and there's no sign of any movement, so we start to move to the chopper, one at a time, just like we're supposed to do.

We run like there's someone chasing us, and we both make it into our new positions before the rest of them move. We watch the area and give them the clear to move.

"All clear, Fire. Move now," Bullet orders them to the chopper, and I watch through my scope. I see movement after they've all moved out of the house, so I take the shot. I hear Bullet begin to shoot and cringe, knowing what this means as I take down at least five more guys. Harris has Al-Quaren, and the other guys are following him, shooting as they move forward.

"Get him the fuck in that chopper!" Kaleb yells. We take two more down, then they begin to run. Harris forces Al-Quaren onto the chopper and shoves him out of the way, holding him down. They all start to jump on around us, and I stay focused on their backs. Kaleb is last in line, and I watch him turn to look when more shots are fired. Men move in quickly, surrounding the last of them, and I shoot as fast as I can, taking out every single one I can get in my view. The rest of the team continues to move, but Kaleb turns to fire.

"Fire, move now!" Bullet yells between shots, and he finally listens and begins to run. I watch the area through my gun and miss how Kaleb lands on the ground. When I pull my scope back to him, he's holding his shoulder and trying to get up before he's ambushed.

"We're being ambushed. We have to fucking go now." I feel Steele begin to lift the chopper.

"Don't you dare fucking leave him." My voice is very loud in my own ear. My demand was heard, and he better fucking listen.

"Go, Steele. Get him the fuck out of here." Kaleb's voice crushes my heart.

"No," I argue, only to have them talk over me.

"We have to go now. We'll all die if we don't get the fuck out of here." The forcefulness of Steele's voice is cold, and I'm instantly pissed. I take out the three men holding Kaleb down, missing him every single time, only to have more grab him. We lift off the ground, and my heart falls out of my chest, smashing all over the ground below. I can't fucking feel. I can't breathe, and panic begins to flood through my veins. We're leaving him. I can't. I love him. I can't breathe. I'm dying inside. They'll kill him.

I work hard to keep my focus on Kaleb for as long as my scope will allow and watch him move his head. He's alive. I send off one last shot and kill the fucker holding the knife near Kaleb's face before I'm no longer able to see him.

There's so much fire in the air and a few hit the chopper, but don't disable us. I stand quickly and move my rifle to the side of Steele's head and hold it point blank. "Go the fuck back, right now, or I'll blow your goddamn head off."

"I can't. We have to get Al-Quaren to the States." I feel a firm grip on my shoulders and a familiar voice in my ear.

"Elliott. We had to move. We were all going down if we didn't."

"Harris. I can't leave him. Make them go back now." Tears fill my eyes as I try to talk around the giant lump in my throat. I can't breathe and only lower the rifle when Harris guides it out of my hands. I fall to my knees and cry as I hear Kaleb for a second in my ear. His guttural sounds almost kill me as I hear him hurting. I wish he would say something to me.

"Fire. Talk to me." I listen for him to respond.

"Ti amo, ghiaccio." I have no idea what he's saying.

"I'm coming back for you. I promise. Stay alive. I need you." I listen for more and only hear Spanish coming through.

"Cierra la boca. Yo te torturo tan lentamente. Te deseo que ya estaban muertos." I don't waste time asking Harris to translate. I want Kaleb to hear me as long as he can.

"Please fight for me. Don't let them break you." The sound in my ears goes silent, but the sound of my heart fills it.

"Harris, what did he say?"

"He said he loved you in Italian."

"Oh my god. Please go back. Please, please, please fucking go back for him, Steele."

"Ice. We will. I just need to deliver him, then we're coming back."

"NO. NO. NO. NO. We're fucking coming back tonight. Drop me, Steele. I can't leave him." I don't recognize my own voice.

"You're not going in alone. We need to regroup and get our shit together. We don't operate like that."

"Fuck how you operate. If you leave a man behind, then I want no fucking part of this team." I reach for the cable that drops us, in hopes of getting it loose before someone has a chance to stop me, but I fail. Harris is standing too close and pulls me into his arms, holding me tight, and I want to kill him right here for stopping me from jumping.

"Harris, let me go. I swear to God, I'll kill you." I pull out my pistol and set it on his temple.

FIRE

Prologue

KALEB

I can hear her in my ear as they pull away. The sound of her voice screaming keeps me fighting until I don't have a choice. There's too many of them. I can lie here and take their brutal attacks all fucking day because I know she's safe. I'll play their games as long as it takes. I'll either die this way, or I'll kill a few of these mother fuckers and find my way out of here and back to her.

I feel the scrape of the gravel across my skin as my body is dragged to god knows where. My eyes are both swollen shut from some assholes steel toed boot to my face. I have no clue where I'm at. I only know there's tiny fucking pebbles digging in to my flesh. I'm not an idiot. I know this is only the beginning of the torture I'll receive.

I feel at least five sets of hands grip my flesh and throw me on the back of a truck like a bag of trash. The landing only intensifies my already bruised ribs, but I welcome the pain. It means I'm still alive.

I focus on the sounds around me, trying to memorize every single fucking sound. There's nothing but the harsh whispers of the night. My focus shifts to the loud cawing scream coming from above. I can hear the vulture circling as if there is something here to feed off of. I refuse to believe that's my fate and silently will that fucker to choke on the next rotting flesh it preys on.

The rumble of the truck engine starting reminds me of the truck we were moved in earlier, but it's slightly smoother. I imagine an old farm truck with a similar bed as I'm flipped to my face so some dickhead can tie me up tighter. The restraints are harsh and I'm trying my hardest not to fight back. I need the element of surprise on my side and I'm positive having two eyes that will open would be a great help.

I start to focus on the movements of the truck as I'm man-handled. The further away we get, the harder it is to swallow. I know it'll be hard as fuck for my team to find me now. My only hope is to stay alive long enough that my guys can find me. They're great at what they do and they will find me. I'm just not sure how long it'll take them. Their first priority is to get the target back to the States under any conditions and if any of them falter from that I'll personally kick their ass myself.

The sound of the truck breaking pulls me back to the reality of the nightmare I'm living. I'm lifted to my feet by the ropes that I'm bound by and shoved face first off the back of the truck. I will kill this mother fucker the second I'm free. I can smell his fucking filth everywhere and will never forget it.

The feeling of my body scraping against the ground again pulls to surface the pain I'm trained to deal with. It doesn't make it easier. I fight the urge to vomit as they drag me into a wooded area. The rustling of dried leaves crunching under their boots on what I can imagine as a stoned filled road burns into my memory. I'm trying to recognize everything I can. I'm hoping like fuck that I'll need this information in the near future.

The voices from their foreign language all ring in my head long after I'm tossed into some sort of cold cemented cell, the metal door is slammed sealing me to my fate for now. These men have no idea who they have fucked with. I'll build my strength in here. My mind begins to run a race of its own. I roll over and spit out the blood that's pooling in my mouth and try not to think about anything but her.

Jade's beautiful skin lights up my memories and even through this fucking hell, I can feel her. I know she's mad as fuck and won't stop until she gets to me. This should be comforting to me, but it scares the fuck out of me. I can handle anything they do to torture me, but if they lay one fucking finger on her it'll feel like I'm being gutted.

I have to keep her inside and safe. She'll give me the strength I need to get through this no matter what my fate is and I know my team won't let anything happen to her. That's all I can do for now. I'll let her be my angel in this hell. She's my blonde haired beauty. The woman I'm falling in love with and she'll be the strength I need to survive.

I hear more voices outside the door and I work to translate their disgusting words that are barely audible to my ears. Chicken shit motherfuckers. My knowledge of how this works should have me shitting myself in fear, but I'll be fucking damned if these assholes will ever smell fear coming from me.

I wish they'd come in here and untie me. Let me have a fair chance against their bullshit. But I know how this works. Most likely I'll be left here to die unless they find a reason to keep me alive. In the grand scheme of things that isn't likely. They can do whatever they want to me. I can spend the last few days of my life knowing I succeeded. I never once faltered my country and given the chance to do it all over again, I would in a heartbeat. There's only one thing I'd do different. I can't change it now and even if I could, I'm not sure how I could stay away.

A tiny tear slips out of my eye and across my nose as I think about the way it should be. I was so close to having everything. My heart is still full and even though I'll most likely never feel her soft skin again, I swear I can smell her right here and now. I swallow hard and acknowledge the reality of this situation. The odds of me making it through this are very slim. I can only hold on to the memories and die with a vision of her in my head.

Their voices get louder and I translate a few of their words. I know they're coming in soon to attempt to get me to talk. I will never talk. I swallow around the large lump in my throat and begin to accept my fate.

I'll die soon with only one regret. Jade.

The next book in the Elite Forces Series – 'FIRE' will release April 26th

Pre-order now for an exclusive early price!

ARC acknowledgments

We'd like to thank all of the blogs who signed up to review our first novel together! We hope you loved it and we can't wait to read your reviews! Thank you so much for joining us during this special release!

Acknowledgements by Kathy

This part is easy for me. I have to thank my partner Hilary Storm for this unbelievable journey we are on.

We are having the time our lives writing together. Even though we write differently, we still fit together perfectly. The way we consume each other's ideas. Focus and plan. Our phone calls, text messages, all of it has been done in a way no words can express. The greatest thing about this is, our friendship has blossomed into one of a sisterhood. I will cherish her forever.

To my husband and children- Day in you hear about my stories. The support, the pride you show me when you honest to god listen will last beyond this lifetime.

To our editor Julia Goda- Snap woman. You are as badass as they come.

To Golden Czermak- The photo god. The genius. Thank you for everything you have done to make this possible for the two of us.

To our cover models Tessi and Dylan- We both look forward to this wild and crazy ride the four of us are about to set sail on. Damn, this is going to be fun.

To our BETA readers- We nailed it you said. Here's to all of you.

To Helena Rizzuto- My friend, my sanity. What can I say, except thank you for always having my back. For jumping on board with this project and running free like the wind to help Hilary and I succeed.

To Lisa Shilling Heinz of The Rock Stars of Romance- You never disappoint me. You are one hell of a business woman. I appreciate you more than you will ever know.

To every reader/ blogger/ author who has shared. Will read. Leave an honest review for ICE. Hilary nor I could do any of this without you. Our work would lay stagnant on our computers. We would have nothing. It's because of you we do. I'm eternally grateful.

To Victoria Ashley and SE Hall. Both Hilary and I are very sorry to tell you that Kaleb Maverick is ours. Although we may share. Maybe!

Kathy's books

The Shelter Me Series
  Shelter Me
  Rescue Me
  Keep Me
  The Contrite Duet
  Contrite
  Reprisal
  The Syndicate Series
  The Wrath of Cain
  The Redemption of Roan
  The Absolution of Aidan
  The Deliverance of Dilan (out April 12th)
  To read Kathy's books click here.

Acknowledgements by Hilary

Kathy Coopmans is an amazing woman and it has been an absolute pleasure beginning this journey with her. I know this series will be epic because every single time we talk.... We enhance it. The story unfolded beautifully as we both allowed the creative words to flow. The lineup we have in mind is going to blow people away and I can't wait to stand proud as fuck right next to you! (Yes I'm the one that says fuck mostly through the book if you haven't guessed lol.)

My husband and kids are my life. Without their love and support I could never do any of this. It is through them that I have learned to love, live, and take chances. My heart is full because of these four.

Golden... My furious man! You have been amazing to work with over the past two years! This series will provide new ventures for us both and I know we'll stand stronger for it in the end! Lots of love my friend!

Dylan and Tessi. My two fav hotties right now! How in the world do you two plan to deal with us? You're stuck with us on this journey and I couldn't be prouder! Everything happens for a reason and I know deep in my heart this collaboration is just the beginning of careers that will flourish! It's through the love and support as a team that we will all conquer great things!

Eric- I have to give you props for the props! I love that you had so much knowledge and allowed us to use yours for this! It means the world to me! You have no idea how much I appreciate our chats. It's great to bounce ideas off of someone like you!

Julia- You made us look good in this! Thanks for your cooperation in making this happen! We're so please to have you on board!

Betas... I want to thank you all for pointing out the imperfections! We loved hearing from each of you and appreciate you taking the time to help make this possible!

SE Hall and Victoria Ashley- My loves! I'm so glad you love Kaleb! We can maybe work out some sort of trade with your guys if you really think you're going to claim him! He's a hot one so bring your best to the table! I know you both have them!

Our loyal followers who will love this and share it like crazy, just like they always do. It is because of you that we keep writing with the urgency we do. We can't wait to share our stories with you so we can see how you react. Thank you for always allowing us to be a part of your lives through our words.

Read more of Hilary's Books

Six (Blade and Tori's story)
  Rebel Walking Series
  In A Heartbeat
  Heaven Sent
  Banded Together
  No Strings Attached
  Hold Me Closer
  Fighting the Odds
  Never Say Goodbye
  Whiskey Dreams
  Inked Brothers Series
  Jake One
  Jake Two
  Bryant Brothers Series
  Don't Close Your Eyes